THE HERO

The gun-carrier burst from the forest upslope, crashing through a screen of brush, an Invader squad strapped upright in the jouncing afterbody and firing toward the house. Michael Wireman jumped up, kept his body behind the angle of the house, and flung grenades into them until the carrier swerved out of control and stalled, and the men in the upstairs windows shot the squad and the choking driver to pieces.

Michael Wireman shook his head. He sighed, softly.

Newsted looked at him. Michael Wireman raised his rifle. Newsted shook his head and grinned wolfishly; he lowered his own gun. "So *you're* the hero," he said, indicating the fallen Invaders.

Michael Wireman looked at the gun-carrier, canted over at an angle, its deck surmounted by the detritus of dead Invaders; at the bundles on the ground at the base of the farm-house, who were Earthmen too stricken to walk; he felt his own body, which could barely stand, and whose face hurt almost unbearably. "Oh, yeah, I'm the hero," he said.

FALLING TORCH

ALGIS BUDRYS

BAEN BOOKS

FALLING TORCH

A Baen Books Original

Baen Publishing Enterprises
P.O. Box 1403
Riverdale, N.Y. 10471

ISBN: 0-671-72033-3

Cover art by Wayne Barlowe

First printing, January 1991

Distributed by
SIMON & SCHUSTER
1230 Avenue of the Americas
New York, N.Y. 10020

Printed in the United States of America

DEDICATION

To Richard McKenna
and Theodore L. Thomas

It is good to have friends.

AUTHOR'S NOTE:

Falling Torch has never been published before in this form. A 1959 version, *The Falling Torch*, was published without the material that appears here as Chapter Seven, and with certain other differences in the text, though the latter are slight.

At the time of the appearance of the earlier version, some critics, while being generally kind to it, offered the theory that it was in some sense autobiographical, or that it wanted to be. This is nonsense, but it is plausible nonsense. I am a Lithuanian citizen, and Lithuania has been occupied by the Red Army since 1940.

But my laughing, charming, vigorous father, and my purposeful, indomitable mother have no counterparts in this novel, and as for me, I neither have prominent ears nor martial or political ambitions.

What I do have is a fascination with how many pyrotechnically successful leaders in history have been strangers to the cultures they came to rule, how many were physically peculiar in some way, how many passed through a major crisis that ought to have destroyed them, and how little their biographers have succeeded in explaining their turns of mind. They were people who did not fit their world, and somehow emerged with the capability to change their world to fit them. A sample list would begin with Genghiz Khan and Timur-i-Leng, and include Napoleon Buonaparte, Abraham Lincoln, Franklin Delano Roosevelt, Adolf Hitler and Josef Stalin, but it could be extended backward and, I rather think, forward in time. Not all history-making political figures emerge from some such background, but it's striking how many of them do, and how often they are the ones who make history in excess.

It was my intention to tackle that ambitious theme in *The Falling Torch*, but for one reason or another that version did not include all the episodes I thought were required to complete the attempt. The book got along very nicely anyway, going through seven printings and staying continuously in print for more than 16 years until I withdrew it from publication at about the time it had quietly sold over a quarter of a million copies in North America alone. For those considering this new version, I give my assurance that whatever caused this popularity is still here, with I hope a little more basic coherence. For the absence of computers, lasers, and digital watches, and for a remarkable general slowdown in technological evolution in the next five centuries, I have no explanation, so I hope you will not notice it.

—Algis Budrys

ALGIS BUDRYS

2513 A.D.

The cortège moved slowly, slowly down the broad white marble esplanade that bent to overhang the inward curving shore of Lake Geneva. Wireman was dead at last. . . .

The Alps cup Geneva and its lake in a green valley. The water is blue and cool; the mountains are gray-faced, triangular, hooded with snow that plumes in faint banners at the touch of the high-altitude wind. In the summertime the lake is dotted with pleasure boats and bounded on three sides by the most fashionable resorts in the human universe. On the fourth side of the lake is the city. It is the capital city of the Solar System.

. . . Because there was no direct access to the lake side of the esplanade except across the paving, and because the police would not permit such a crossing today, every onlooker at Wireman's funeral procession stood with the city rising like a heritage behind him. And he faced not only the parade of mourners and the military bands, not only the whining gun-carrier with the flag-draped

1

teak coffin mounted on its turtleback in place of the usual automatic cannon, but also the lake, the mountains, and the April sky. . . .

Geneva is white, built so at Wireman's behest. The architecture is Modern Neoclassic, which the best architects decry with some justice, but which is the closest approach in stainless steel, glass and planed limestone to that Grecian ideal which has been irrevocably planted in the human mind as the proper form of a public building. The low, rectangular structures sweep around the curve of the lake, descending from the green foothill slopes, and most people find the city's beauty breathtaking. There are three human-inhabited planets in the Solar System, supporting a population of over four billion altogether. Geneva is the symbol of them all. Above it, on the blank face of a mountain, is Wireman's chalet. The snow-plumes wreathe it in draperies that sparkle with the sun. The glass walls are lightly tinted to cut the glare; a carefully measured gradation of pigment leaves the lower halves of the windows perfectly clear, and a man sitting in the great leather chair beside the stone fireplace can look out over the edge of the world.

. . . The military bands marched down the esplanade in funeral step, playing the old, hallowed dirges. At times, when the music affected them, the members of the crowd could be seen to sway back and forth, like frost-darkened barley left standing in an abandoned field. But there were no outcries. The crowd was silent in any ordinary sense. There was no sobbing, and no real grief. The news cameramen had no difficulty finding enough footage of men and women with handkerchiefs to their streaming eyes, but in terms of the total crowd—the terms in which Wireman had thought—what these people felt was not grief. Grief is one of the refined emotions. It is dependent on the prior presence of a raw, primary feeling: loss. It was loss these people were feeling—irreparable loss. They dressed it in various guises; love, but also fear, stolidity, nervousness, and suppressed elation. A beehive deprived of its queen does not feel grief. It is conscious of deprivation. It buzzes. Over the people and over Geneva hung a murmur compounded of all the muffled noises a subdued crowd uses to express its component emotions. Sighs and gritted teeth, shuffled feet, grunts and coughs of sorrow or anger and laughter filled the cup of Geneva's valley, trembled over the ice-blue water, and thrust against the mountains. . . .

Geneva is white, clean, modern yet vaguely derivative of the past, built to a grandly-conceived overall plan which was scamped in the end because of practical difficulties, but not where it would matter to anyone confining himself to the main streets and districts. It is a graceful, happy city. It has traditions, carefully cherished, extending back to the old Swiss city which was partly destroyed in the Invasion. That city is gone now, utterly supplanted. There are those who remember that the Invaders had rebuilt it before they were driven out during the Liberation, but, however that may be, Wireman had the new Geneva built upon it, and the old traditions furnish a satisfactory foundation for the new reality.

A human city.

. . . In the government buildings, there was complete silence. The civil service clerical personnel were out in the crowd. Only a few offices were in use; private offices, where men were sitting alone.

In one of those offices, the man who would take Wireman's place as administrator of the human universe looked at his desk clock, saw that soon he would have to leave for the waiting tomb on its promontory overlooking the lake, and stood up. He was a young man, in his middle thirties, and he had an air of unerring efficiency about him. He had a number of cultivated mannerisms and personality traits to disguise the air in public, or at least misdirect the eye away from its true nature, but he was not yet practiced enough to maintain this cloak when alone.

He went to the window and looked out. The cortège was three-quarters of the way along the esplanade, and would be at the tomb shortly. Wireman's heir had perhaps five minutes before he had to go downstairs to his car and be driven to the scene of the interment.

The young man looked from the cortège to the pinpoint sparkle of the chalet, and thought:

"Only he could have gotten away with that. I'm a professional. I know what I'm doing, and I know what has to be done to lead people. I'm aware of my responsibilities, and I think I'm in the right.

"He was an amateur. He never worked his way up like I've had to. He would have lost out the first time he tried to play intra-departmental politics. Lost out and gone to oblivion. But he began at the top. He couldn't have known as much about political mechanics as I do. I or a dozen other men in the other departments around here. But if *I* tried to govern from up in that eyrie, I'd be a tyrant with delusions of grandeur. They'd stone me to death.

"It's not ability. He made mistakes—plenty of them. They gave him time to correct them, where they wouldn't have waited on anyone else.

"It's not popularity. There are always a few who'll love you. He had no more of those than usual. But they depended on him. And he excited them. Just driving by, wooden-faced, in the back of that car of his. They shouted themselves hoarse; the women fainted left and right in the crowds. But he wasn't one of them. They couldn't love him.

"It's not fear. I thought it might be, until I saw how he'd quietly block that secret police chief of his. And the chief died, and wasn't replaced by anyone much, and the people's attitude never changed.

"It's not clever advisors. The Secretary of State who framed the new constitution for him didn't live long enough to see how the old checks-and-balances wouldn't work, after a quarter century of Invader indoctrination. Wireman revised it all, and re-revised it, until it's a model of efficiency now.

"No, it was something in him, and I don't suppose I'll ever have it. He learned something, somewhere, somehow—he learned it in his bones. I'll be the best they've got, but they'll know I'm no Wireman. Mine will be the Earth to shepherd, and everything that's in it, but I'll never be a man, my son. Not like he was."

The young professional looked back down at the cortège. Walking behind the gun-carrier were Wireman's official heirs: the cabinet members, the leaders of Congress, the bureau chiefs.

The young professional smiled. They, too, had their plans, but they had all missed an essential point. They were plainly identified in the public eye as subordinates. They were too far up the ladder to be rising young men; too well branded as not having enough ability to wrest position at the very top. In six months, in a year, they would all be gone.

The rising young men were in their offices, each of them aware of his abilities and his chance, each protected by his ideal position; too far down to be tarred by anyone's brush, too far up to be shunted aside. Each of them was aware of his rivals. An invisible network of awareness radiated from office to office, like a web of lightning.

Wireman's heir pondered the concluding passages of the latest and supposedly most penetrating Wireman biography. He had studied the book minutely after its publication last November, and committed a great deal of it to memory:

> Irascible at times, withdrawn always—even such an archaism as "crotchety" must be pressed into the service of his description—dour, tough; all these qualities are part of Wireman. His face is as familiar to us all as the face we see in our mirrors each morning. His voice comes to our ears without an instant's hesitance for recognition. We cheer him as he passes among us, the famous unbending figure ramrod-stiff and motionless in the Presidential car—The Old Snapping Turtle, Willoughby the cartoonist christened him for our generation—alone, always, without advisor or aide. The final authority. The lawgiver. The iron conscience of us all.
>
> We know him. We know what he gave us; our humor, our freedom, our self-respect when these were all but lost—*were* lost, so much so that we no longer even missed them, 'til he

restored them to us almost singlehanded. Without fear, without prejudice, with out hesitance—and perforce without friendship, too, or even close acquaintance—he dominates the history of the Earth and its dependencies without rival in past or future, for what hero could but repeat Wireman's accomplishment?

And yet, who knows this man? Even now, at the twilight of his life, age has not softened him. The forces that made him what he is, the solitary agonies that shaped the granite of his nature, the torments, the triumphs—the defeats that must have been, to temper him to such a hardness—all these are lost, unchronicled, ungossiped, unguessed. The record is there, in the lines of his face and the rigor of his gaze, but only there. What is it that shapes such a personified force? What makes of a man, born of woman, a man greater than men?

It may be we shall never know. We can only be grateful that we have him.

—Robert Markham, Litt. D.

Wireman's Time, Columbia University Press New York, 2512 A.D. $4.00

Wireman's heir turned away from his office window. In Wireman's personal copy of Markham, the flyleaf was slashingly pencilled in the old man's characteristic hand: "Poppycock!"

What was a man planning to assume Wireman's place to make of that? How did a man grow into such a mold?

Wireman's heir left his office, took the elevator, and got into his waiting car. Other cars were just beginning to roll away from curbs all along Government Row. Other young men sat in the back seats of their cars; other young men very much like this one. The quiet, gliding cars passed and re-passed each other on the broad street that led toward the tomb. All the young men were frowning thoughtfully.

ONE

1

Fifty-four years earlier, and four light-years from Earth, there was a wall telephone in the main kitchen of the Royal Cheiron Hotel. When it rang, one of the potboys answered it and Thomas Harmon, the supervising chef, paid it no attention. He was tasting a sauce one of the underchefs had prepared. He rolled his tongue to let the more important taste buds at the back of his mouth give him their judgement. Twenty years here, from potboy to his present position, and he hadn't been a young man when he began. But his taste had only improved as his other senses slackened and lost their distracting vigor. He was a good chef—not quite as good as his reputation, perhaps, but good.

The underchef was looking at him anxiously, out of the gold-flecked brown eyes that had already, in these few centuries since the colony's foundation, emerged to mark the difference between Earthmen and Centaurians.

Harmon nodded slowly. "Good," he said. "But I'd add a little more jonesgrass, I think." Jonesgrass wasn't quite thyme. But thyme didn't grow on Cheiron, which was Alpha Centaurus IV. Jonesgrass would have to do. "Just a touch, Steffi."

Steffi nodded respectfully, his face relieved. "Just a touch. Right, Mr. Harmon. Thank you." Harmon grunted pleasantly and moved on to the next underchef.

"Excuse me, please, Mr. Harmon." It was the potboy who'd answered the telephone. Harmon turned his head sharply:

"Yes, boy?" His tone was more snappish than he would have liked. But interruptions threw him off his stride. And now he recalled the ring of the telephone, and that annoyed him further. He was rather sure of who it would be, calling in the middle of his workday like this.

"I'm sorry, Mr. Harmon." The boy's expression was just properly intimidated. Harmon smiled softly to himself. It wouldn't do the boy any harm. Any good chef was a bugbear to his help, for at least one good reason. It gave apprentices an appreciation of the master's status, and firm self-confidence when they finally achieved his station for themselves. Also, it weeded out the flustery hearts before they had an opportunity to do something asinine in the middle of a busy hour.

"Well?"

"There's—there's a call for you, sir. They say it's important."

"No doubt," he growled. But since he suspected who it was, he went to the phone. And he'd been right. It was Hames, President Wireman's Chief of Protocol.

"Mr. Prime Minister?" Hames asked punctiliously.

"Yes. What is it, Hames?"

"President Wireman has asked me to inform all cabinet members he's calling an emergency meeting for seven o'clock. I realize that doesn't give anyone much time, sir, but the president asked me to stress that it is important, and to ask everyone to please be prompt."

"What is it this time, Hames? Another resolution to be read into the record of the Centaurian Congress?"

"I'm sure I don't know, sir. May I inform the president you'll be at his apartment on time?"

Harmon frowned at the telephone. "Yes—yes, I'll be there. I'm sworn to serve the interests of the Government in Exile, after all." He hung up. And the hotel wouldn't be discharging its famous Mr. Thomas for taking a few hours off, so that was all right. In the end, all Hames's call meant was that anyone ordering dinner at the Royal Cheiron tonight wouldn't quite get the best in the exotic Terrestrial cuisine for which its kitchen was famous.

So, no one on Cheiron being qualified to judge— except for the handful of refugee Earthmen—there was no apparent loss to anyone. Harmon found himself resenting it just the same. He called over his head assistant, informed him bluntly that the dinner hour was in his hands, and went to his suite to change.

The suite, as befitted his position on the hotel staff, was well-situated, and the bedroom was comfortable to the final degree. There was an adjoining sitting room, furnished with a stiff luxury that both complemented the grace of his bedroom and made it difficult to use. Harmon generally stayed out of it, preferring to keep the adjoining room as another badge of rank, rather than as anything intrinsically useful. He was ten years a widower, a man of habits as confined as they were educated, and he had no need for more space than his bedroom gave him—which was a good deal in itself. He knew the suite was his for as long as he cared to stay. That would be true even after his faculties had stiffened to a point where his most useful contribution would be his name at the foot of the dining room menu.

He took down the suit the hotel valet had placed in his closet this morning, and laid it out on the bed. Dressing slowly, reacting pleasurably to the touch of soft, expensive, perfectly tailored fabric, he reflected on the usefulness of what, on Earth, had been a slightly eccentric hobby.

He studied his reflection in the closet mirrors. Spare, with a little pot belly and a distinguished sweep of white hair, he could have passed easily for the man entitled to own the Royal Cheiron, rather than a member of its staff.

He picked up his room telephone and asked to have his car brought around to the side entrance. While he waited, he reminded himself there was a wedding banquet scheduled for next week. He spent the time roughly blocking out a menu for the affair, engrossed in the delicate business of balancing the flavor and texture of one dish against the next, reminding himself to consult with the wine steward before he made any final decisions.

2

He drove slowly to the part of Cheiron City where President Wireman lived. From time to time he looked up at the pale blue sky, with its yellower sun and faintly-seen smaller moon. He had never quite tired of the sight, for reasons that had changed through the years of his life on this planet. At first there'd been the attraction of unfamiliarity, and he'd gazed like a goggle-eyed reuben from the back country farms looking up at his first tall building. Then, after the strangeness had worn off, he'd been on the night staff at the hotel—an awkward, fortyish man who wasn't at all sure of himself, trying to do a young boy's work, often feeling like a dolt as he stumbled over the frequently impenetrable accent that had crept over the language here. In those days, he'd been grateful for the sight of dawn.

Now he drove through narrowing streets and thought of how far beyond Cheiron's sky Earth and the Solar System lay—of the really unimaginable distance that separated them.

Four hundred years ago, this had been Man's earliest foothold on the stars—earliest, and, as it developed, only. In four hundred years, the passage time had been worked down from ten years to five, to very nearly the Einsteinian limit on speed through three dimensions, but that was the best they could do. They were tinkering with an ultradrive just before the Invaders hit Earth. They had it now, but it was too late for the Solar System. Centaurus was the focus of the human race today, and Earth, like the Western Roman Empire, was only another backwater region in a sprawling foreign domain.

It wouldn't have mattered in the end, Harmon thought to himself. Once the colony had taken hold, every century was another step toward this day whether the Invaders had ever come or not.

The Centaurian System Organization not only covered its own solar system but stretched out its own colonies, trafficked with races and systems far beyond Earth's touch, and loomed so large in its own right that the Invaders hadn't dared strike at the child over the parent's corpse.

His car hummed precisely to itself as he turned the corner of the street where Wireman's apartment house stood, in a neighborhood that had slipped badly. As he parked, behind a car he recognized as Secretary of the Treasury Stanley's limousine, he saw Secretary of Defense Genovese draw up in a taxi, pay the driver, and wave the change away. Harmon crossed the street and met Genovese in the threadbare lobby.

"How are you, John?" Harmon said.

"Hello, Tom. How're things?" They shook hands, a bit awkwardly out of rusty habit, and made small talk waiting for the elevator.

"How is your wife, John?"

"Fine, Tom—just fine."

"Business good?"

"Couldn't be better. I started working on a big account today. If I land it, the commission from it'll just about put Johnnie through school all by itself."

"Well, that's very good news. I hope you get it. Where're you sending him? I understand the city university here is very good."

"That's what I hear. But he's holding out for KenLi—that's in Areban, the one with the good engineering school. It's an awfully long way away —he won't get home except for Christmas and summers. But, if he really wants to go, that's his business. He's big enough to know his own mind. Of course, there's a girl going to the liberal arts school at the same university—that may have something to do with it." Genovese chuckled.

They got into the creaky automatic elevator together, and rode up to President Wireman's floor. The hall was narrow, and badly lit. Harmon always felt uncomfortable, waiting out here, trapped in a tight enclosure walled by featureless, brown-painted doors, all alike; so many secret panels hiding activities that were best kept tightly locked away; plans and schemes that would wilt if ever taken out in the air. Genovese pushed the doorbell.

Hames answered the door, holding it open wide and flattening himself against the wall of the narrow corridor that led past the kitchenette. "Mr. Prime Minister. Mr. Secretary of Defense. The rest of the cabinet is already in the living room. President Wireman will be with you in a moment."

"Thank you, Hames," Genovese said, stepping aside to let Harmon go first, and Harmon reflected on the change that always took place in them when they came here; the sudden weight of dignity that formalized their manners and modulated their voices. He walked into the living room, with its carpet and furniture all wearing out, with the springs sagging in the couch and armchairs, and the nap gone off the upholstery.

We come in here, he thought clumsily after the manner of an infrequently witty man, and we assume the gravity of another world.

Puns, he thought, meanwhile bowing his head in acknowledgment as the other men in the crowded room left their seats to shake his hand and murmur greetings. Young Takawara was quite fond of them, I remember. If he could make them work out bilingually, so much the better. He was clearly the best of my assistants. I wonder what happened to him, on that last day when everything was so confused and we barely got off and fought our way through the Invaders' ships.

We were all so much younger, then. We were all so relieved that at least the president and his cabinet were able to get away. We would have waited for the others if we could, but we thought we had at least saved the most important people. We were wrong. We left the only ones who mattered when we left all our Takawaras behind.

Stanley had saved him a place on the couch. Harmon took it thankfully. "How are you, Mr. Secretary?"

Stanley was about his own age, dressed in a slightly more conservative suit than his own, but one of equal quality. They shared tailors, and Harmon's account was in the bank Stanley managed.

"Quite well, thank you, Mr. Minister." Whenever they happened to meet ordinarily, Stanley called him Tom. "And you?"

"Quite well." He looked around, reflecting the questions of health were becoming less polite and more literal every day. There was Yellin, paradoxically the Secretary of Health and Welfare, sitting stooped over his cane, his yellowed hands clasped over it and his rheumy eyes looking off at nothing, dressed in shabby clothes and cheap black shoes. Next to him was Duplessis, who might have been his brother—a little younger, a little more active, but only a little. He pictured them living in their furnished rooms, hermits in gloomy little caves, debating whether the day was warm enough for them to shuffle painfully downstairs and out to a park, day after day through all these years—perhaps regretting they'd ever come to Cheiron at all—old before the Invaders came, and lost here on this foreign world that held nothing for them.

Hames came out of the corridor leading from the bedroom. "Gentlemen, the President of the United Terrestrial and Solar System Government."

They all got to their feet—a roomful of old men.

Ralph Wireman, when he came in, looked no younger.

3

He was a thin, slump-shouldered man. Harmon noted the worn look of his clothes—the subtle discoloration that years of perspiration had made in the dye, and the limp hang of cloth that had stretched to his movements and rubbed thin until no cleaning or pressing could make it hold its shape.

He was a tired man. His black hair had receded, thinned, and turned white. Deep creases ran down his hollow cheeks and formed folds under his long jaw. His nose had sharpened, and the corners of his mouth had sunk into his cheeks. His lips were faintly blue. The lean vigor that had been his characteristic had disappeared completely, turning into stringiness and set, stubborn, determination. The last time Harmon had seen him, his eyes had still been feeding on a buried core of vitality. But tonight even that last spark was gone, as though the final watchfires of an encircled army had gone out at last.

"Gentlemen." His voice breathed up through his rattly throat.

"Good evening, Mr. President," Harmon said, wishing he hadn't come.

"Good evening, Tom."

The rest of the cabinet now said "Good Evening" in rough chorus, and once that was over they could all sit down, with Hames standing watchfully beside the president's chair.

I wonder what it is tonight? Harmon thought. When they had first come to Cheiron, these meetings had had some kind of life to them. There had still been purposefulness in those days: conferences with the local government of Cheiron, meetings with the officials of the Centaurian System Organization, finances to be arranged out of what Solar System funds had been available in credits here before the collapse—it had been a busy time. But it had been a waning life, and after all the organizational procedures became cut and dried; after the invitations to address the Centaurian Congress had dwindled down to resolutions never read but simply inserted into the Record, bit by bit stagnation had crept over them all.

In those early days, there'd been hope. They'd even thought the Centaurians might go to war with the Invaders and make Earth free again. But the Centaurians and the Invaders had been a bit too closely matched—so closely that no one could predict an outcome. And the Centaurians had been a long time away from Sol. The links had grown thin. Their language, four years away from home by radio, had drifted toward the foreign. Their interests, taken up by the enormous frontier of their own interstellar sphere of influence, had turned away. Their memories of Earth, four hundred years outdated, had legendized to watery sentiments of a dim and distant, archaic little world they looked back on, sometimes, but would not trade for the ravage and destruction that were the risk of losing to the Invaders.

The Government in Exile was twenty years older, now. And men who'd been middle-aged were something more than that today. Even Genovese, the youngest of them all; the bumptious, unsettling Boy Wonder, was one of them now.

Harmon looked at Wireman's eyes again, and wondered if it was finally all over tonight.

But Wireman didn't bring it out immediately. He clung to the old pattern of cabinet meetings, wanting to hear the usual preliminary reports that were still being given as they had been when Geneva stood and an army of clerks had been busy preparing digests and critiques of the week's events.

Harmon looked from Yellin to Duplessis to Asmandi to Dumbrovski—from Health to Postmaster General to Labor to Agriculture—and it was like peering at phantoms.

"Edward?" Wireman breathed.

Stanley got up. His papery cheeks twitched, and he shrugged. "There's nothing new. The Centaurian government has unblocked the usual month's dribble from our assets. I made the usual application to have the sum increased, and got the usual answer that the series of Invader government claims against Terrestrial assets here is still being adjudicated. In short, they're keeping us going but no more than that. They don't want to give the Invaders any solid bone of contention."

Wireman nodded painfully. "Karl?"

Hartmann, the Attorney General, stood up as Stanley sat down. "The Invaders' latest claim is being reviewed by the Centaurian Supreme Court. I filed the usual brief quoting precedents against allowing it."

"I think it's clear," Wireman said. "The legal situation bears no resemblance to the *de facto* state of affairs. The Centaurian System Organization is sympathetic to us, but it would be folly for them to go to war with the Invaders for our benefit. If, at some time, Centaurian and Invader interests clash sufficiently to cause a war, then we may expect the Supreme Court to suddenly discover precedents conclusively in our favor, and for all manner of other wonderful things to happen for our benefit."

The same familiar treadmill, Harmon thought. We stay alive, and after a fashion we continue to function. Or perhaps we don't, anymore.

Hartmann was back in his chair, and now Wireman straightened a little.

Here it comes, Harmon thought in expectation.

"Gentlemen . . ." Wireman's voice was very old, and very tired. "We're approaching an unexpected crisis." He looked over at Harmon, plainly asking for help, but Harmon still had no idea of what kind of help he needed. A Prime Minister was a man who could help under any circumstances but these. So long as Wireman was still alive, it was he who represented Earth, who was the symbol of something gone twenty years to ruin but still alive as long as he was. Only if Wireman were to go would Harmon again have a function, and weight. Wireman's weight. Harmon dropped his eyes helplessly, and after a minute, Wireman took up the fraying thread.

"We know—we've always known—that if the Centaurian System Organization could find some way to help us without becoming overtly involved, it would do so. The paradox, of course, has always seemed insoluble. But it no longer is."

Harmon raised his head quickly.

"As you know," Wireman continued, "the Liberation Fund has been maintained through all these years to keep open a line of communication with resistance groups on Earth. It has always seemed to me of paramount importance that we do so, even though the cost of maintaining the necessary ultrafast scout ship has been a crippling burden on the fund. Without those few radio contacts which the ship has made from time to time, we would be completely cut off from our home and our people. Up to now, we have never been able to do any more. Such groups as we were able to contact were small, ineffective, and hopelessly scattered. But recently, one dominant, highly organized and well-led group has emerged. I refer, of course, to the one led by former Lieutenant Hammil, who has requested and will be granted the rank of General.

"Even so, I have never entertained any great hope. General Hammil's group could not be anything but a nucleus against the day when outside help could be provided—help which we were in no position to send, and which no other government could supply without risking war with the entire Invader empire.

"But, only yesterday, I discovered that for the first time since our arrival here, we are in a position to make a positive move toward Earth's liberation. Briefly: the Areban Automatic Weapons Company, which is a major supplier of the Centaurian System Army, has just received a contract to manufacture a new type of automatic rifle. As a consequence, its contract for the present type has been cancelled—and it has on hand a large stockpile of completed weapons of the earlier type, all new and in perfect condition, for which it has no conceivable market anywhere within the boundaries of the C.S.O. I was approached by their agent, who told me that his company will supply these weapons to us together with suitable ammunition, on speculation against the day when a liberated Earth will be able to pay them. In short, gentlemen, we can perhaps be free again."

Harmon had never seen him look quite so tired, or so hopeless, as he did after he finished.

Yellin took an audible, quavery old man's breath. The end of his cane scraped over the carpet. For a moment, they were all a little paralyzed. In another moment, they'd all be talking at once. But Wireman said, "Tom, I'd like a private conference with you and John," and the outburst choked. Hames bent over to help Wireman out of his chair, and Harmon saw Genovese getting to his feet, looking thoughtful. "I'm afraid we'll have to go in the kitchen," Wireman said in his dignified, apologetic way. "Mrs. Wireman is resting in the bedroom."

4

The kitchenette pressed in on all sides of them with its cement floor, rust-stained sink, and peeling cupboard doors. Wireman sat on a newspaper spread on the dusty, narrow marble windowledge, and after he sat down he looked up at Genovese with a mixture of pain and wry amusement. "Now you can tell me I'm crazy, John."

Genovese leaned uncomfortably against the sink, his lower lip pulled back between his teeth. He shook his head. "It won't work, Mr. President. Never in a million years. Automatic rifles against an empire. Granting initial successes based on

surprise—granting the Invaders have pulled out
their combat troops and sent them to some other
frontier—what happens when those troops are
brought back? No—never."

Wireman looked at Harmon. "Is that your opinion, too, Tom?"

Harmon nodded, feeling the oppression of the
narrow room, looking at the ancient stove on which
the wraithlike, thin-voiced Mrs. Wireman had to
cook.

Somewhere, Wireman found a smile to bring to
his exhausted face. It was like watching a man
smile on the rack. "You're right, of course. After a
month or two, their reinforcing fleet would reach
Earth, and that would be the end of us. And
yet—do you believe that fairy tale about the arms
contracts? The sudden oversupply of weapons? The
idiot company throwing its products down a rathole?"

Harmon grunted. His shoulders jerked erect,
and he brought his knuckles down sharply on the
edge of a shelf. "No! No, by God, of course not!
Sorry, Ralph—I'm getting out of practice, I guess.
The Centaurian government's making a move at
last!"

Wireman smiled faintly in agreement. "That was
my analysis. Officially, they're not involved. But
they're giving us the means to get things started,
and I think if we do well at all, we'll see the
heavier weapons and motorized equipment flood-
ing in remarkably as though someone, somewhere,
had worked out a logistic schedule years in ad-
vance and disposed C.S.O. fleet units accordingly."

Genovese laughed suddenly—a yip of pure excitement that Harmon would have thought the
years had buried. But Wireman did not smile. He
sank back into the tired, hopeless desperation that

only his underlying stubborn streak kept from lapsing into total lifelessness.

Harmon couldn't understand that. Looking at this kitchen, picturing this apartment, he thought about Wireman living out these past twenty years, waiting for this day—living them out here, trying to hold out, to live on the pittance he could allow himself from the trickle of available money—watching men no older than himself find positions in civil life and live comfortably while he had to stay here, keeping a symbol alive, trapped into being President of the United Terrestrial and Solar System Government, watching his family eat cheap food and dress in patched clothing, and knowing that even Prime Ministers could find ordinary work and bring no tarnish to the bright memory of Earth's freedom, but that the President could not. The rest of them could admit in public that Earth was no longer there, but someone had to preserve the fiction—someone had to embody the legal fable that the Government in Exile still represents its people—and Wireman was the man. So why, today, was he more weighed-down than ever?

"Tom—"

"Yes, Ralph."

"Tom—and you, John—" Astonishingly, Wireman was almost pleading. "You'll back me with the rest of the cabinet, won't you?"

"Back you? Of course, Ralph." Harmon frowned, perplexed.

Wireman sighed and moved his hand over his face as though wiping away cobwebs. "Thank you," he whispered.

Harmon looked at Genovese, raising his eyebrows. Genovese shrugged, shaking his head. It made no sense to him, either.

"All right, gentlemen, I think we'd better rejoin the others," Wireman pulled himself together and stood up slowly. He smiled feebly at Harmon. "A man my age ought to be in a hammock on a back lawn, somewhere, watching the grass grow."

Harmon followed him back into the living room, and Genovese hooked the kitchenette door open again behind them. They took their seats.

The rest of the cabinet was completely still, watching Wireman, occasionally glancing at Harmon and Genovese to guess what had gone on between them. Harmon kept his features still, wondering what Wireman was going to do.

"Gentlemen—" Wireman began. "I assume you've all had time to think over the implications of my announcement."

Harmon doubted it. He'd seen how rusty his own thinking was. He doubted if any of them could be much sharper, and in the case of several of them—Yellin, Duplessis, a few others—it seemed obvious that good judgement was something beyond their present capacity. But every man in the room nodded, honestly enough, for every man's judgement confirmed to him that he really had thought everything out to its final conclusion.

It goes, Harmon thought. Bit by bit, it wears away from disuse and no man can say where it went—but it's gone, and too far to bring back. But we're all there is available; we'll have to do it somehow, tired as we are.

He wished desperately that Takawara had gotten away. He wished this had happened ten years ago. He wished there'd been time to gather them all in—all the bright, young people who would be at their peak today. But history never really bends to any one man's wish.

"We have our chance at last," Wireman continued. "We mustn't spoil it. All our energies, all our efforts, will have to be devoted. There'll be administrative work to do, a definite program to be shaped and put into effect. We'll be conferring with the Centaurian government again, I imagine. There'll be one more load. In addition, once the rising on Earth has fairly begun, we'll all have to be ready to go back to Earth at a moment's notice. Under the circumstances, considering the transportation difficulties, it might even be advisable to be in space, waiting."

Harmon heard Stanley, beside him, grunt in annoyed surprise. And gradually, as he looked at the rest of the cabinet members and saw Wireman's words being digested, he saw most of the other men's faces change.

5

"Just a minute, Mr. President!" Stanley said testily, getting up.

Harmon watched Wireman's eyes as he looked at the Secretary of the Treasury, and now Harmon could understand what had troubled the president so much. There were many things in Wireman's look. Surprise was not one of them. "Yes, Edward?" he said with a sigh.

"As I understood it, you're asking us to devote full time to this project. Is that correct?"

"You're a member of my cabinet. You're sworn to uphold the Government, Edward." It was said quietly, and it broke the bubble of Stanley's temper.

He waved a hand uncomfortably. "Well . . . yes. Yes, I am. But, just the same, I've got a position here—a rather important position—I've got responsibilities. . . . Damn it, Ralph, I'm the manager of the biggest bank in the city!"

"I see. Do you mean that you can't leave your outside job immediately, or do you mean you consider your responsibilities as a banker more important than your obligation to Earth?"

Karl Hartmann was on his feet. "I think that what Secretary Stanley means is he's let down roots here. It's—after all, Mr. President, it's been twenty years—it's a little difficult to suddenly break off all ties. In my case, for example, there's my law office, my home . . . why, my wife has spent ten years furnishing and decorating our house. My son is married to a girl here, and they have children of their own. . . ." Hartmann's glance wavered under Wireman's. It was his turn, now, to become progressively angrier as he stumbled harder. "After all—after all, when I came here I had nothing. I had the clothes on my back and nothing else. I worked, Ralph—I worked very hard. I had to learn the law all over again. I had to clerk, and I had to pass Bar examinations—at my age. Back on Earth, I was a pretty good lawyer. That didn't count here. I had to start all over again. I made it. I'm a pretty good lawyer here. And if I go back, what'm I going to do—take my exams for a third time? The first thing there's going to be is a new election. D'you think I'll be in the next president's cabinet?"

Harmon, thinking of his years scrubbing pots, working his way up, thinking of his position now, hard and fairly earned, heard most of the other men agreeing with Hartmann.

My God, he thought, we never realized—none of us—we never thought of how we'd really feel when this day came.

"That's a very interesting attitude, Mr. Hartmann," Wireman said tightly, fighting back with no sign of the weakness he'd shown talking to Harmon and Genovese; not giving an inch. "I don't think it's completely shared by other members of this cabinet, most of whom are in situations analogous to yours and Secretary Stanley's." He looked over toward Genovese, and only Harmon saw the clutch of his hand as his fingers closed tensely in the narrow space between his thigh and the edge of his chair. "For instance, I'd like to hear what John has to say."

Genovese was looking down at the floor. He didn't move or raise his head. Wireman tried and failed to reach him with his eyes. Genovese took a deep breath.

"Ed Stanley asked if this was going to be a full-time project, Mr. President. And you referred to his 'outside job.' I think we've got the crux of the thing right there." His voice was low and halting. "Now, I promised you something a while back, Mr. President, I'm not forgetting that. I made that promise as a member of your cabinet. But now I've got something to consider. What Karl said, expressed the spot I'm in. I'm a machine tool salesman in a territory that covers all of Cheiron City, Belfont, Newfidefia, and the little towns in between. I spend six months a year on the road, at least. I make good money, because I learned how to sell. I work hard—I'm not trying to build myself up by saying that: here's the point—I spend all day, every day, being a salesman on Cheiron, for the Cheiron City Machine Tool Works. Except that once or twice a month, when I'm in town, I come up here for a few hours. Now— which is it that's the outside job?

"I want you to understand, it's not that I'm unpatriotic or that I don't remember what they're going through, back on Earth. I've got my share of relatives back there. If I was back on Earth, I'd take a gun and do what I could, no matter what it cost me. But—"

"Shame!" Yellin broke in. "For shame! I have never heard—I had never thought to hear—treason spoken in this room!" He was trembling with rage, glaring from Genovese to Hartmann to Stanley.

"You are all summer soldiers!" Duplessis shouted in echo. "While this was a—a lodge where you could play at government, you were content to do so. But now that there is work to be done, you're leaving it to us—the ones of us you've sneered at. You in your fancy foreign clothes, talking in that barbarian accent and forgetting every civilized custom. Well, go—go back to your banks and briefs and traveling salesman's routes! Go back to your greasy pots! We don't need you! Those of us who remembered our homeland and waited for this day will do it for you—old as we are!"

There were others: Asmandi, Dumbrovski in his slow-speaking way, Jones—the room was full of angry men on one side or the other. Harmon looked at Genovese sitting head down in the midst of it, letting Stanley, Hartmann, and the others who felt the same way, argue it out with Yellin and his side. Harmon felt sorry for him, startled by the dull gray color of his face.

"Gentlemen!" Wireman was still holding himself in. His tight lips were almost invisible, but his voice was under good control as he turned to Harmon. "We haven't yet heard from our Prime Minister."

Harmon could feel the pull of his eyes across

the room. They faced each other, both motionless in their seats, while Harmon remembered his early days on Cheiron, with Nola sick and lying alone in her room at night while he went out to work. And then she'd died, and somehow he'd still gone out to work, because it wasn't in his nature to starve or sit. Now he had his position, and his suite, and his reputation.

It was going to be terribly hard, getting this cabinet to pull together. They were working on a chancey plan at best—if it failed, that was the end of them as a functioning group, and the end of hope for Earth, perhaps, and yet they were almost bound to fail, divided among themselves, shot through with bitterness and shame, worn out to begin with—What was a man to do?

"It's my intention to stay with the president and work with him," he said after that long moment, knowing it was probably a terrible mistake. "I gave my promise." The temptation to do the opposite had been very strong. Hartmann had been right—even if they succeeded, there was nothing for them on Earth to compare with what they had here.

Wireman bowed his head for a moment and slumped in his chair as the tension drained out of him. Then he raised his head. "Very well, gentlemen, you've heard what Tom had to say. Now I'd like a vote—how many of you are in favor of proceeding with the proposal to arm General Hammil?" He looked around expectantly. Harmon looked with him—and winced.

Then he sighed quietly and wondered what he'd gotten himself into. A clear majority of the cabinet was opposed. The division seemed to fall precisely along the line separating those who'd been able to make careers on Cheiron and those who, for one reason or another, had not. He felt exposed, with only old Yellin and the other recluses to count on. It was not his natural side of the fence at all. He'd have to fight the very men he understood and was friendly with, and consider as allies the men with whom he'd had nothing in common for twenty years. More and more, he was oppressed by the knowledge that they were all weak to begin with—that there were not enough of them for the work, even united—and now, he knew beyond almost all possibility of doubt, they could only fall.

He would try it—he'd promised Wireman and he'd sworn an oath a long time ago. Every logical faculty he possessed told him it was hopeless, and he believed in his own logic. But, he would try it, however unwillingly. He'd do his best to patch this up, and go on.

Then Wireman said: "Very well, Tom, I'm asking you to form a new cabinet from among Mr. Yellin's group. As for the rest of you, gentlemen, I'd like your resignations." His face was ashen. "I have no choice."

Panic-striken, Harmon suddenly realized there were some bargains he could not keep.

The room had fallen completely silent. In that silence, Harmon said: "Ralph! You can't do it!"

"I have to, Tom. I have to have people I can count on."

"You can't form a cabinet with six members. You can't bring in anyone new—we're practically all there are of us, right here in this room, and the rest didn't even have the tie of the cabinet to hold them to Earth. Those of us here have all got to work on this together, somehow. Six people just

can't do all the necessary work—not six people as
tired as we are. It can't be done. It's almost—yes,
it *is* suicide! And certain failure, too."

"We'll *have* to do it. This is more important
than our overworking ourselves. This is for Earth,
and Earth's freedom. Each of us has to be depend-
able. Each of us is going to have to carry this thing
through."

Harmon shook his head in disbelief and murmured: "We stayed together for twenty years while
there was no hope. It took the chance of winning
to break us up."

"Tom, have you changed your mind about staying
with me?"

"Ralph—be reasonable!"

"I am reasonable. More reasonable than you, it
seems to me." Wireman's neck seemed unable to
hold his head erect, and he rubbed it wearily.
"But, perhaps, you've grown away toward a different kind of reasoning from mine. All right—Mr.
Yellin, I'll ask you to please form a new cabinet."

6

They were filing quietly out through the narrow
corridor—Hartmann, Stanley, Genovese, and the
rest, with Harmon bringing up the rear. Harmon
tried not to listen to what Wireman and the others
were discussing in the living room. Suddenly, affairs of state were no longer his concern. He moved
in a shell of his own, vaguely noticing that the
others ahead of him weren't talking to each other
but were simply, as quietly as they could, leaving
the apartment. When Hames touched his arm as
he passed the kitchenette doorway, it took him

some little time to react. Then he said: "Yes?" He didn't recall what Hames had said.

The Chief of Protocol repeated it. "I beg your pardon, sir. Your final salary check—will you want me to assign it to the Liberation Fund, as usual?"

Harmon nodded quickly. "Yes—yes. And, here . . ." He took out his billfold and handed Hames most of his cash, doubling the amount of the check. "Add that to it."

"Yes, sir. Sir, you know *he* has to go on whether he wants to or not."

"I know. Goodbye, Hames."

"Goodbye, sir."

"Come in for dinner, sometime. Compliments of the house."

"Thank you, sir. But I'm afraid I couldn't do that, now."

"No—no, I suppose not." He stepped out into the crowded hall, and Hames shut the blank brown door behind him.

When the elevator came, there wasn't room for all of them. "Go ahead," Harmon murmured. "I'll take the next one down." He waited, alone, wondering whether Wireman would somehow make it work, after all. He didn't wonder where he'd see Hartmann or Genovese again, if ever. Possibly, there'd come a time when they could meet each other again. Or perhaps they'd all simply disappear into Centaurian society, never to re-emerge as anything but Centaurians with no distinction from all other Centaurians.

The elevator came back and he took it downstairs alone, standing rigid in one corner, his hands clenched on the bumper bar, momentarily certain

that the car would never stop and that his entire
life had been spent in it, greasily sliding down the
blank-faced shaft, the process interrupted only by
the equally inexorable coincidences of the car's
wired-glass porthole with the wired-glass portholes
of the never-opened hall doors, the passage too
swift for any real sight of the world beyond the
shaft, and all his memories of the past only a
hallucination designed to protect his sanity. He
felt as old and as crippled as Yellin. He felt helpless and ignoble because he had not, in the end,
been able to rise above his human nature.

He had thought better of himself than that. All
his life, he had known better than to expect or
desire continual selflessness from others. He had
conceived of himself as one of the few in each
generation who must rise above the flesh in order
that the great majority would not be called upon
to do so. He had made the choice early, knowing
that by doing so he was giving up his heritage as a
man enjoying his humanity. He had learned soon
enough afterward that, in spite of his best efforts,
the life of the average man still was not without its
difficulties. But he had believed, nevertheless, that
without him and men like him—without the rare
men like Wireman who were even better than
himself—the life of the average man would cease
being merely ordinarily difficult and would become nearly intolerable. But what was he to think
of himself now?

The car continued to slip downward.

Then it occurred to him that he was too concerned with his personal feelings now—that he
must see this thing in its historical perspective,
not as the decline and fall of Thomas Harmon and
Ralph Wireman, but of all they had ever repre-

sented. He must see that what had happened to them as individuals was painful, true, and regrettable, but that it only reflected what must have happened to the ideal of a free Earth.

It was hopeless from the day we left Earth, he thought. We were under the delusion that we were saving more than ourselves: that we were a symbol on which the hope of a suffering people could focus—a star to watch for in the dark of night, in hope of what it might bring tomorrow. But we were wrong. People tend to believe that the symbol is the thing itself, yes. People can believe that so long as Ralph Wireman lives, so long as there is a group calling itself the government of free Earth, that a free Earth does, in fact, somehow continue to live on. But also the people do not believe in these things, for the people are wiser than anyone knows. They wait, but they can't wait forever. They have to live their day-to-day lives. The Invader, standing there on the corner is more real than the President five quadrillion miles away. The Invader is always young, always trim, always efficient. The President is growing older, and the promise of his return is never kept. The faith grows thin and dim. And each man in the end falls back upon himself to work out his own destiny, and then all faith in greater things is lost, at last, forever.

I'm sure back on Earth they don't believe in us any longer, no more than we believe in ourselves. No matter how much or how little lip-service they and we might still pay. And in the backs of our minds, we always knew it. That's why the ablest and most vigorous of us started to be drawn away from the moment we touched this world, and only the old and ordinary stayed because they had no choice but to keep hoping—to nourish in themselves that thing which is no longer hope, but desperation.

And so on Earth we are forgotten, except by the crippled and the ineffectual. The war is lost, and the times have changed—we are gone, and we know it. Freedom is gone, and Earth knows it. And there is no hope for us, no hope for Earth. The vigorous Invader rules the streets, ever young, ever renewed, while we here have no one to replace us.

The elevator stopped at the lobby floor, a few inches out of alignment. Harmon seemed to need all his weight to push open the door, though actually it moved easily enough.

And Wireman knew it better than any of us. He must have. He must have known it before we even got aboard the ship. But he went anyway. For our sake?—for Yellin and me, because we'd feel better for a while before the hope died or soured? For his family's sake? For the sake of whatever brief hope Earth might have, to sustain it through the first years of Invader consolidation? For any and all of those things, I suppose. What a conscience he must have! Even here, he couldn't let himself drift away with Genovese and Stanley and Hartmann and the other young ones of us—even though he was the best of us all. He wouldn't be a broken man today. He wouldn't be threadbare. And he must know that. But he was our president, and he had to live out his lie. The people are wiser then they know, but they don't know it. There was no escape for Wireman.

But why should I be ashamed because there was an escape for me? The world is full of practical people who have made practical choices and are respected. I am respected. By all.

Harmon let the elevator door close behind him and began walking out of the lobby, thinking of how he was respected by nearly all. Then he noticed that there was someone sitting in one of the lobby chairs.

It was a tall, hefty, somehow soft-looking boy whom Harmon knew to be in his middle twenties. It was hard to believe—so hard that the remembrance had to come by means of a deliberate process of reconstruction: twenty years of living here on Centaurus, over four in flight from Earth, and the boy about a year old when they all hurried aboard the ship. So he was twenty-five or six, this man/boy.

He sat in the hard, upright, scarred, cheap lobby chair with his shoulders and back slumped forward, his forearms pressing into the tops of his thighs, his limp hands dangling between his knees. He stared down at the floor between his feet, and little twitches of expression; tremors at the corners of his mouth, widenings and narrowings of his eyes, fleeting contractions of his jaw muscles, all flicked on his face like the sounds from a randomly spun dial's radio. Whatever he thought was always reflected on his defenselessly expressive face, and, obviously, he thought in rushes and chaotic jumbles, his glands struggling to keep up with the fantastic number of emotional cues this brain must thrust upon them.

There was something wrong with him, Harmon thought, a little appalled at the lack of organization, the absence of discipline in that mind. Somewhere, somehow, that mind had failed to make contact with the world.

"Hello, Michael," he said, and President Wireman's son looked up.

7

He had his mother's dull brown hair and eyes, and her sharp-chinned features. The only thing he seemed to have inherited from his father was the shape of his ears—the famous jughandle curve that had been a good personality touch in Wireman but was faintly laughable in his son.

"Hello, Mr. Harmon." The boy—Harmon saw it was impossible to think of him as a man, chronology or no—had a colorless, unsurely pitched voice. He looked up with a sort of shy friendliness. "Is the meeting over? I saw Mr. Stanley and Mr. Genovese leaving."

"You didn't speak to them?"

The boy shook his head uncomfortably. "No, I didn't."

Perhaps they had ignored him. It was easy to do. Speaking to him was uncomfortable for both sides of the conversation. Harmon himself would have gone by him quietly—Sidled by him guiltily? Harmon suddenly thought—if this were not the last time they were likely to meet.

"Yes, Michael, the meeting's over. But Mr. Yellin and some of the others are still there."

"Oh. Then I suppose I shouldn't go up yet."

By tacit agreement, he was never home during cabinet meetings. It was an arrangement that seemed to have simply worked itself out without need for planning. A small boy is not, after all, an asset to a conference of state. By the time he was older, that habit of absence was too firmly established.

Harmon, who never visited the Wiremans so-
cially now that his clothes and position in life were
an obvious embarrassment, had consequently seen
very little of the boy. In the first years of the
Government in Exile, there had been so much for
Wireman and the cabinet to do that the boy had
naturally been little more than a figure vaguely in
the background. Harmon knew nothing of his rela-
tions with his parents now. But he had the impression that Michael was a disappointment to his
father—more than an impression, by all logic—and
that the boy's childhood had largely revolved around
his mother. Though whether the latter was the
result of the former, or vice versa, Harmon did
not know. He remembered dimly that aboard the
ship, where Michael had changed from a baby to a
boy, he had been bright and lively—too lively,
perhaps, with his constant clamoring intrusions on
his father's valuable time. Certainly, that much of
him had changed, or been changed.

He spoke now in a perfect Centaurian accent,
showing no trace whatsoever of his origin. Even
his clothes which, being inexpensive, were neither
styled nor shaped according to the latest local
fashion, were nevertheless worn in the indefinably
different way a Centaurian would wear them.

"Is something new happening?" Michael Wireman asked.

New? Even this boy, then, Harmon thought,
realized they had settled into a rut. One word, and
he had summed up the politics of a government
twenty years maintained with nothing to govern.

Harmon thought over his answer. "Well, I think
you might be going back to Earth, soon."

"You mean the Centaurians are finally going to
do something?"

"Let's say they're going to help you help your-selves."

Michael looked at him in surprise. "Won't you be with us?"

"I'm . . . afraid not, Michael."

"Don't you *want* to go, Mr. Harmon?".

"I—" Harmon shook his head.

"Don't you miss it? Don't you want to see it again?" The note of surprise in Michael's voice was turning into frank incredulity.

"To be honest, Michael—"

"Do you *like* living here? Do you like these people, and the way they are?" Swept up, the boy wasn't even listening to Harmon any more. He seemed to be genuinely enthusiastic, personally excited, for the first time since Harmon'd known him. It was obviously the topic in which he was much more interested than any other.

"The way they are?"

"*You* know what I mean. They're rough, they're impolite, they're pushy . . . they're nothing like the people on Earth."

Harmon took a deep breath. "Do you know a lot about Earthpeople, Michael?"

The boy flushed. "Well—of course, I don't re-member Earth." His animation checked itself for a moment. Then it rushed back redoubled, as these things will. "But my mother's told me all about it and all about what life there was like. She's shown me all the pictures she has of all the places on Earth—all the big buildings, and the museums, the libraries. She's told me all about Fifth Avenue, and the Arc of Triomphe—" He stumbled over the pronunciation. "—And Geneva, and Rome . . . all those places."

"I see . . . You know, the buildings weren't any

bigger than some of the ones here. And there are some rather good museums in this city."

"I know. But nobody goes to museums here."

"Yes—well . . ." Harmon was powerless. What reality ever took the place of a lifelong dream? What words, what persuasions, could ever hope to controvert an emotion?

"Do you really think there's that much difference between Centaurians and Earthmen?"

"There must be!" Michael Wireman exclaimed. "Look at their history. They came here in the first place because they couldn't find places for themselves on Earth. They were either misfits or opportunists. Instead of trying to assume their responsibilities as members of a civilized society, they ran away.

"What can you expect of a society built by the descendants of people like that? They'll work—of course they'll work, each of them for himself alone, not thinking of his fellow man at all—and they'll push their technology—why shouldn't they, with the planet so rich and full of resources just waiting for the first lucky entrepreneur to stumble over them—but is that all there is to life? Thinking of nothing larger than yourself, filling the world with shiny gadgets and roaring machines, and nothing else?

"What kind of heritage do they have? What kind of ideals? What kind of education? Yes, some of them are pleasant. Some of them are likeable. Some of them don't take themselves as seriously as all that. Some of them can even see that things could be better—but they're swallowed up in the mass; they don't count for anything in the face of their society."

Michael Wireman's face was flushed. He seemed

to be waiting now for Harmon to argue with him—
Did he, perhaps, *want* to be argued out of his
convictions?

Thomas Harmon shook his head slowly. What
could be done with this individual? He had already lived a quarter of a century. Could it possibly seem to him that a half century more would
teach him to change his mind about so many things?
And here he was, far from all he believed in.
Neither fish nor fowl—drowning in water, flop-
ping helplessly on land—my God! Harmon thought,
what *could* he be but what he is?

And what am I to do—say a few magic words to
him, and make him different?

In one flash of empathy, Harmon suddenly understood what had made this person. The pressure
of overwhelming events had made him, had caught
him, had not only shaped him but overwhelmed
everyone responsible for shaping him. Defeat—
unacknowledged defeat, defeat called by another
name because the adult around him could not bear
defeat—had made him what he was. And what,
Harmon thought, what else has made *me*?

"Michael—"

Harmon stopped. Had he been going to say the
magic words? What were the magic words? There
was no magic in the world of men. There was
history, which is the politically biased record of
past political events. There was psychology, which
is the internal politics of the individual. Sociology:
the study of the effect of politics. These were what
any man knows of people, of what has been done
with people, of what can be done with them. And
politics, as he had long ago grown bored with
hearing quoted, was the art of the possible. And
only the possible. What was possible for Michael

Wireman? For Ralph Wireman? For Thomas Harmon?

"Michael—"

"Yes, Mr. Harmon?"

What am I doing? Why do I insist on finding the magic answer for us all, when there is no such thing? Though we may all of us well need to find it.

"Michael—" for the third time.

"Would you like to sit down, Mr. Harmon?" the boy said, concerned for him.

"No. No, no, I'm all right, Michael . . ." He found that he was trembling with frustration. Yet he could not stop demanding of himself that he somehow solve everything—solve all the insoluble problems.

And then, quite abruptly, he said: "Michael . . . I wonder if you would come upstairs with me now. Right away."

"Upstairs?"

"I—I've had a thought. I think perhaps it will help your father . . . and myself . . . with a certain . . . problem." Thomas Harmon turned and thrust himself toward the elevator with awkwardly controlled excitement and a desire to move things rapidly—to launch events into motion before there was time for doubt or turning back. He had set his mind to a problem, and his mind had given him an answer because it must. It might not truly be the answer he had demanded, but his mind could not let him see that.

They might do it, Harmon was thinking. With the boy, they just might do it. A new symbol, sustained by a magic name. Wireman might just agree to it particularly if Harmon offered to come back. Harmon could stand Yellin. He could stand anything, give up anything—if he thought he could succeed. He could not let himself again fall prey to doubts and torments. The boy *must* be the answer!

Monarchial succession, in this century? Harmon snorted. That was a ludicrous idea. But to people— the people who were so wise, but so ready not to be—might they not very well mistake a new Wire- man for the vigorous extension of the old? And wasn't it true, after all, in a way? And what did it matter that the few Earthmen who might learn better could not possibly offset the effect of the name on the great majority who would not? Time was all that was needed; a little time, and a briefly enthused population, and after the power of C.S.O. troops and ships would be there, and the old Wireman, before the bubble burst. Surely the boy would *want* to help, in whatever way he could.

Neither fish nor fowl, nor good red meat, but a new pair of shoulders for Wireman's weight. Youth, energy—surely there was energy there, waiting to be released at the proper demand—there must be—above all, there was undoubtedly desire . . . Yes, yes, surely this was the best solution within the bounds of the possible.

The boy. Yes. What did it matter, *what* he was? It would be *who* he was that would count, for as long as was needful. "Hurry, Michael!"

He turned to look. The boy was following, plainly hesitant, but plainly intrigued, plainly wondering what it was that waited to receive him.

TWO

1

A dark earth waited to receive him. Michael Wireman waited for the hatch to pop open, knowing that the scudding spaceship would be very nearly at drop altitude. He wondered what the Invader radar stations were making of it. He looked through the porthole again, seeing nothing but darkness, thick clouds, and the faint orange straight-edge of a starboard fin that was only just cooling down from their entry. There was nothing below him that he could see—no mountains, no forests, no gleam of moonlight on water.

He turned sharply away from looking out and tightened the straps of the bulky load fastened to his back. The view from the port was hardly pleasant for a man about to jump out into it with a seventy-five pound load added to his own weight, and nothing to help him but a flimsy-looking whirligig which, collapsed at the moment, stuck up above his head like a folded umbrella.

He set his wrist altimeter from the repeater dial on the bulkhead beside him, played his flashlight on it to charge the luminous dial, and hoped everything would work out all right. On Centaurus, when Thomas Harmon first broached this idea to him, and his father reluctantly agreed, he had been eager to do it. In training—with instructors who were certainly members of the Centaurian armed forces but were careful not to say so—he had done well and grown confident. But it was dark and bottomless outside, and though he yearned to return to Earth, now he was aware of the tall trees and sharp rocks waiting for him below—if, indeed, there was anything there at all.

He was nudged from behind, and turned to see Isaac Potter smiling at him whitely. It made him feel instantly better to see the pudgy little man, looking squashed under his own load, crowned by his own bumbershoot. On Cheiron, Potter had been equally determined, if unspurred by Michael Wireman's special eagerness. On Cheiron, the tubby technical representative had said: "I go where the guns go," and meant it. He still meant it, no doubt, but at the moment he, too, was obviously very much aware of Earth not as something beautifully drawn on a wall map but as a solid body with teeth.

The spaceship was full of noises. Air friction shrilled through every plate and stanchion. The thrumming of the motors vibrated Michael Wireman's teeth. Every joint and angle of the ship was creaking out its own particular note.

"Ready?" Isaac Potter shouted over the noise.

Michael Wireman grinned back. He smoothed the flaps of his crash helmet down over his stubborn ears and buckled them under his chin. He

made sure his rifle was strapped securely to the
pack.

There was a dinging noise from beside him. He
looked at the illuminated plate that had been rigged
beside the hatch. The word "Brace" was lighted.
Under it, "Fire" was still dark. He dropped to a
sitting position, curled his arms around his knees,
and laid his head down on his thighs. There was
no room for irresolution. If he weren't braced
when the pilot fired him out, he would go pin-
wheeling across the sky, a broken doll. That had
been stressed in training, and demonstrated with a
dummy. He felt the tips of Potter's boots against
his buttocks, and knew the other man was also in
position.

He reminded himself, quickly, that once he was
out in the air the best position to take was an angle
of forty-five degrees relative to the ground, face
down and body straight. That way, the vanes of his
chute would stand less chance of breaking off. It
had been explained to him in training that this
never happened. He had then been told what to
do to keep it from happening. There were a few
jokes, apparently stock ones from the C.S.O. armed
forces, about what position to take if the vanes
broke.

The light clicked on under "Fire." The dinging
noise now became a clamor. The hatch popped
open, and suddenly he and Potter were out.

His next coherent thought came as he hung in
the clouds, vanes whirring over his head. A dozen
yards above him, and opening the distance slowly,
was Isaac Potter. Michael Wireman had no idea
whether he'd done things properly or not. He
looked about him and saw nothing but clammy
darkness. His ears were full of the sound of his

breath in the oxygen mask over his chin. The ship was gone, back to the friendly spaces outside the Solar System, and whether Invader radar had made something of it or not, it was now too late for anyone to do anything.

He looked at his altimeter. The needle was unwinding rapidly. Still, he did not dare look away from it.

The ship's pilot—yet another hired Centaurian civilian with suspiciously military mannerisms—had guaranteed to put them within a mile of the rendezvous with General Hammil's partisan army. He seemed to know all about this kind of operation, and everyone had been satisfied with his assurance. But Michael Wireman had reflected, once or twice on the fact that no one on Cheiron, either Centaurian or Earthman, would know for months how this had come out. He glanced down, looking for the tops of trees. He saw nothing, though his altimeter was down below the one hundred foot mark now. He set his legs to take the shock, and buried his face in his arms.

He hit, and the weight of his pack threw him over. Bruised by stones and scraped by branches, he lay with the breath knocked out of him. He heard something bulky fall through the trees near him, and then the thump of Potter's landing. Whether they were anywhere near where they ought to be or not, at least he and the Centaurian were together, and overabundantly armed.

He struggled to his feet, laden with a pack never meant to be carried any great distance, pulled off his mask and drew in deep breaths. The air that filled his lungs was beautiful—thick, moist, and redolent of pine. A wind caressed his face. He knelt, took a handful of loam, and squeezed his fist around it.

This is my home, he thought. This is my native place.

Once, when he was a small boy still aboard the ship drumming toward Centaurus, he had awakened in the middle of the night to hear his mother crying and his father talking in a loud, strained voice. He had sat bolt upright in his bunk, shocked into motion and alertness without really waking up, and he had listened with wide, staring eyes at the words coming through the thin aluminum partition between his cubby and the main cabin. It was the first time he had ever heard his parents quarrel; the thought that they ever could now came to him simultaneously with the fact, and when he was twenty-five he could remember it with as much clarity as though he were still four, still listening in the darkness, his sleep-swollen lips parted and trembling.

"But, Ralph, what will they *think?* What will they *say?*"

"Margaret, people are forever saying things about something or the other. You can't satisfy them all—it's a mistake to try. The thing to do is to do the best you can for them, no matter what they say."

"And the best thing to do is to resign? Leave them without a government?"

"They've *got* a government, Margaret! The Invader government. If they don't like it, they can do as much to change it as I can. More. They're there. I'm not."

"You're their *president*, Ralph! I—I've never heard you talk this way. I don't understand you!"

"I've had four years to think of it. We've been on this ship all that time, and I don't suppose the world's blown up while I was out of touch. If I'd stayed and the Invaders had never come, there'd have been another election two years ago. I wouldn't have run again. Who's to say I've a right to speak for Earth? My God, Margaret, they're entitled to work out their own destiny!"

"How *can* they!"

"Good lord, I don't know, Margaret! But the invasion's an accomplished fact. Whatever they can do has to be planned from that standpoint. If they pretend it never happened, can I possibly make intelligent decisions? If they pretend it never happened, can they? No—no, I did what I could during the war, and it wasn't enough. It was a mistake for me to ever get aboard this ship. I should have stayed with them. I should have shared whatever happened to them afterward, and *then*, maybe, I'd have the right to make plans for them."

Now, but not then, Michael Wireman could recognize the voice of a divided man. Now, but not then, he could recognize the sound of silent hours spent in thinking, in re-assessing, in slowly giving around before the growing knowledge of a nearly irretrievable error made with perfect certainty of mind.

Then young Michael Wireman had pushed back the blankets and burst out of the cubby, panicked by the thought that something had gone wrong with the world—that for some reason his father would not fix it.

Michael Wireman could still clearly remember his parents' startled face—his mother's pale and shaken, his father's harried and set.

He had flung himself into his mother's arms,

screaming in fear. "Mommy—Mommy!" he had cried. "Don't let Daddy make me be afraid! Don't let Daddy make me be afraid!"

Clasped in his mother's arms, his face buried in her dress, he had not been able to see his father's face.

He let the crumbled soil seep through his fingers, and went to find Potter. The slow tears tracked down from his eyes.

2

No one had come to meet them as yet. They had dug under the roots of a big tree and buried their drop equipment, strewing the newly turned earth with pine needles, and now they stood waiting back to back in the darkness. This had always been the weakest part of the plan. If they did not contact General Hammil's army, their mission and their lives were wasted. But no one had been able to suggest anything better. Certainly, landing the spaceship had been out of the question. Even entering the atmosphere had been a risky business.

"If we stay here much longer," Michael Wireman said over his shoulder, "we'll have an Invader patrol on us soon."

"Yes, but if we move, then Hammil won't find us. I'm not sure what we ought to do."

Michael Wireman listened to the sound of the trees. He heard nothing else. "We'll give it another ten minutes. If we don't hear anything coming by then, we'll move off a little. If we *do* hear anything, we'd better make damned sure of who it is."

"It seems to me an Invader patrol would probably land by helicopter. They can't very well have foot patrols permanently stationed on every mountain in the world."

"Unless they're expecting us. For all we know, Hammil's been captured and questioned by now."

"In which case," Potter sighed nervously, "I don't suppose it matters whether we're caught or not."

Maybe not to you, Michael Wireman thought.

When he saw the silent figure loom up before him, he started. "Liberty," the hulking stranger croaked.

"Weapons," Michael Wireman whispered out of a clenched throat.

"Good enough," the immense man said, still with a husking voice. "I'm Ladislas. Lemme take the bundle off you." Ham hands worked surely at the buckles on Michael Wireman's shoulder harness.

"I'm . . . glad to see you," Michael Wireman said lamely, possessed by a feeling that his first meeting with a free Earthman ought to be an occasion.

"Let's get moving now and shake hands later," a new and decisive voice said from beside Potter. "Here—I'll take your pack, little man." In the darkness, Michael Wireman could just make out a wirey shadow that was probably even a shade smaller than Potter. "My name's Newsted. Let's go."

They moved rapidly among the pine trunks, with Ladislas in front and Newsted bringing up the rear, behind Potter. The pine needles lay thick under their feet, and they made almost no noise. Occasionally Michael Wireman or Potter scuffed a boot. Neither Ladislas nor Newsted said anything when it happened, but their annoyance made itself felt. Trotting behind Ladislas's broad shadow, Michael Wireman began to feel useless and clumsy. He hoped that would pass.

Once, they stopped. Newsted flickered forward past Michael Wireman like a ghost, and touched Ladislas's biceps. The big man put his mouth close to Newsted's ear and apparently said something, though Michael Wireman could not hear him from ten inches away. Newsted nodded and drifted back, touching first Michael Wireman's shoulder and then Potter's, turning them around. They backtracked for two minutes, and no one's boot scuffed. Newsted stopped them again, and explained into their ears, in a throaty whisper that had no sibillants: "Man over dere. No bidnidd being dere. But 'e don' know about ud." Then they swung out in a wide semicircle, and presently they reached a short and shallow valley which Michael Wireman decided must be a fold in the mountain's general slope. Now there were other men around them, who could be felt more than seen in the scrub underbrush that choked the valley. Ladislas put out a hand to stop them, scratched at something, and lifted a mass of brush out of the way. Newsted nudged them forward. Ladislas replaced the brush. Someone snapped on a battery light set down on a scuffed steel radio transmitter, and Michael Wireman found himself in a shallow cave, blinking at a bullet-headed man dressed in a gold-braided tunic, royal blue riding breeches, and polished boots.

The man's entire scalp was stubbled, as though he had shaved it some five days before. So was his jaw. He had coarsely handsome features, eyebrows the color of bleached straw, and icily blue eyes. A reddish moustache grew over his upper lip. He was holding an automatic pistol at the level of Michael Wireman's belt, his finger poised on the trigger.

"Who are you?" he asked in an annoyed voice.

"Michael Wireman. This is Isaac Potter."

The man nodded shortly. "Good. Where do you come from?"

"Cheiron, in the Centaurus system."

"And what do you have for me?"

"Weapons. You *are* General Hammil?"

"Self-appointed as of the moment, yes. Lieutenant Hammil, Terrestrial Land Army Reserve, if you want my commissioned rank." Now that identifications had been disposed of, Hammil shed his grimness and assumed a certain bluff heartiness. He tossed the pistol carelessly onto the radio. "The President's own son, eh?" he said. "I'm honored." It was doubtful whether he was or not. "Well, we'll try and make you comfortable."

"I came here to fight," Michael Wireman said, a little nettled by Hammil's attitude. The man had known who was coming. His little scene had needed playing only if he wished to establish an immediate ascendancy, and Michael Wireman had been prepared to grant that without question. Hammil was the experienced man here. The only thing Michael Wireman expected was a chance to carry one of the automatic weapons he'd brought, use it, keep his mouth shut, and only then, if he proved good enough, to be given whatever responsibility he earned.

"Yes, of course," Hammil was saying. A lightning smirk curled his mouth, and accustomed lines cut themselves into his cheeks. He was not the most likeable man, Michael Wireman decided. "Did you bring my commission?"

"I have it here." Michael Wireman took the envelope out of his coveralls, and Hammil almost tore it out of his hand. He ripped it open, pulled out the parchment, unfolded it quickly, and held it up to the light. He stood with his feet apart, toes pointed outward and the commission held up at arms' length. He seemed to gain stature for a moment, and the shadow he cast in the rays of the single lantern was enormous. He was, Michael Wireman realized, a domineering man by nature. But at this moment his personality was nothing short of awesome. There was the inescapable impression that the bounds of the cave could not contain him; that soil and rock would burst asunder and leave him overmastering the world, towering on this mountain. Then he grinned, revealing rotted teeth.

"Full General," he chuckled. "General, by God!" His thick forefinger moved under a specific line of writing. "General Commanding, United Terrestrial Army of Liberation! Hah!" He chuckled again after his snort of satisfaction. The sound echoed animally in the cave. "It may be thirty years between promotions," he bayed, "but they *do* come when they come! Signed and sealed by the President of the Government in Exile, and delivered by his son! Ladislas—Newsted—come have a look at this!"

He thrust the parchment out at them. Newsted looked at it expressionlessly. "General, all right," he agreed. Ladislas grunted.

Hammil pulled the commission back, folded it carefully, and eased it into the breast pocket of his tunic. "Now let's look at the guns."

"I have a letter for you, too," Michael Wireman said. He pulled another envelope, this one much bulkier, out of his pocket. "It contains a general policy outline, and your orders."

Hammil grimaced at it, took it, and stuffed it into a side pocket. "Thank you," he said shortly. "I'll read it later."

Isaac Potter had opened one of the packs of disassembled rifles. He stripped the canvas back with a quick gesture, like a magician snatching the curtain away from a miracle. Automatic rifle halves lay nested inside each other, gleaming blue-gray in the light. With them were the solidly packed, flat-sided steel bottles of compressed propellant. They had told Michael Wireman, during his training, that each of those little half-pint flasks held enough liquefied gas to move a brick building twenty feet if released at once. An instructor had fired one out of the barrel of a mortar, and it had bounced innocuously over the ground. Then he had walked up to it, jammed one flat end tightly between the roots of a tree, and cracked the valve. The tree had gone over as though wires had pulled it down on hinges.

Oh, yes, they had weapons on Cheiron.

"There you are, General," Isaac Potter said. "Fifty in this pack, fifty in the other. When I signal the ship, tonight or tomorrow, you get the rest." He picked up two halves, slipped a propellant bottle into the butt, and locked them all together with one smooth motion. The assembled rifle seemed to have almost sprung to life of itself. He handed it to Hammil. "The assembled weapon weighs a pound and a half, complete with clip and propellant, exclusive of ammunition. Each propellant bottle holds five hundred charges, and you saw how quickly those may be replaced.

"This model has been chambered for .235 caliber rifle ammunition, since you told us this was the most easily available type. The clips have been adapted, and will hold fifty slugs of that size, with the case and powder charge removed. This is not, of course, a true automatic weapon in the sense that the discharge of one cartridge actuates the mechanism for the firing of the next. It is, rather, a continuous-fire, continuous thrust, propellant-operated, multiple load, short-range infantry carbine, but—" he smiled whimsically, "at Areban Arms we don't often make that distinction in ordinary conversation."

"Pretty," Hammil grunted, weighing it in his hand. He gestured toward Newsted's rifle. "You can see what junk we're armed with. But light. Very light."

"A pound and a half, General. But the problem of recoil absorption does not come up severely, since the thrust is continuous and uniform down the length of the barrel. A blowback valve in the groove just short of the muzzle cuts off the thrust before any is wasted. You will find it a serviceably accurate weapon, as well as one with considerable shock power. The muzzle velocity is quite high."

Isaac Potter, Michael Wireman thought, seems to have found his element with a vengeance. I wish I could find mine.

"All right," Hammil growled, "we'll see. It looks simple enough. It had better be. We've no gunsmiths, and there aren't any rebuilding shops."

"Let me assure you, General, these weapons have been fired after a month's immersion in salt water, and after having been dragged through mud. Until quite recently, they were the standard arm in the Centaurian System Organization infantry."

"And what kind of war did *they* ever fight?"

Newsted asked with a drily corrosive voice. Isaac Potter pinched his mouth together and said nothing.

Michael Wireman couldn't let that pass. Potter was only doing a job.

"The C.S.O. has done its fighting, now and then," he said. "If the government of twenty years ago made a mistake, the current one is coming to realize it. These weapons wouldn't be here if it weren't. I think we ought to remember that."

There was an unexpectedly cold pause. Hammil sucked a tooth. Ladislas simply looked at Michael Wireman, but Newsted's gaze was flat, and unblinking. "We ought to, eh?" he said. Michael Wireman had no idea of what he'd done wrong, but it was devastatingly plain that he'd stepped into a pitfall as bad as Potter's.

"Gentlemen, please," Potter said with nervous vehemence, "I have to stress that the Centaurian System Organization has nothing to do with this venture. The Areban Automatic Weapons Company, as a private corporation, is disposing of a stock made surplus by the armed services' order for a new model weapon. That is all that is involved here, and as a citizen of the C.S.O., I must urge you to make the distinction. We cannot risk enmeshing the government in a diplomatic crisis." He blinked his eyes at Hammil. "You must remember that if the government *does* become embarrassed, its easiest remedy would be to refuse exit permits for the spaceship. Should your only transport be shut off, and Areban Arms having signed only a Freight On Board contract with the Government in Exile, you can see that your supply of weapons and parts would be interrupted forthwith."

Everybody's attention had shifted back to Potter. Michael Wireman relaxed gratefully. These were touchy people.

Hammil looked steadily at Potter and sucked his tooth again. But he had been forced back on the defensive. The little technical representative, for all his nervousness, was for the moment a sparrow who had made a jackdaw take thought. It came to Michael Wireman that Potter had incidentally insured his own immunity from further recriminations. It would be Potter who judged whether Hammil was conducting himself discreetly or not. No one here could afford to antagonize him overmuch.

It also came to Michael Wireman that he shared no such immunity. If he, in all innocence, happened to antagonize these sensitive people again, he could expect to be made to feel it.

Obviously, he must do his best to settle into their pattern as quickly as possible. Otherwise he would go on making mistakes without realizing it. These were Earthmen, like himself. He had to ensure that he would be accepted by them.

"All right," Hammil was saying, and the way he said it was carefully tailored so that he might either have been recognizing Potter's position or simply shifting topics. "In the morning, Potter, I'll expect you to instruct the men in using them."

"I could help with that," Michael Wireman offered. "I've been pretty well trained."

"Oh, have you?" Hammil said.

"Yes, I have," Michael Wireman answered with some sharpness. "I can pass every C.S.O. armed services standard." He was measurably proud of the way he'd taken to training. Through some combination of heredities, he had turned out to be a born rifleman. It was the first intimation, in a withdrawn and unathletic life, that he was under it all equipped with some surprisingly good survival traits. The discovery was recent enough so that he was also measurably sensitive to having it questioned.

Hammil cocked an eyebrow toward Newsted. "Take him out in the morning, Joe. Find out what he can do."

Newsted nodded, and looked at Michael Wireman with a cold smile. He said nothing.

2

There was nothing but dark mist overhead, and it was cold. Newsted had found a spot for Michael Wireman to sleep, beside a bush on one slope of the valley. He had taken him there, and left him there. Even in his coveralls, Michael Wireman could immediately feel the cold dampness begin seeping inexorably through into his flesh. Now he huddled under the brush, his knees drawn up and his arms folded across his chest, mummy-fashion. The cold was gnawing at his marrow. There had been a blanket in his small personal pack—woven to meet C.S.O. armed forces specifications, if lacking a government issue number—but certainly it had never been intended for climates like this. It had turned into an icy, clammy shroud. Still, the cold was even more unbearable without it. The towering pines which had whispered and sighed with the breeze earlier in the night were motionless and dripping.

He heard someone coming toward him, and turned his head, discovering that it was closer to dawn than he'd thought. He could make out a slight figure. It was either Newsted or Potter.

"Michael?" It was Potter.

"Yes?"

"I'm glad I found you," the Centaurian said, unfolding his own blanket. "If I must spend the night trying to sleep in the open, I'll feel better near someone else to whom it's all new. These people don't go to any great lengths to make one feel at home, do they?"

"No—no, they don't."

"But then, they'd naturally be tense and over-wrought. I wouldn't take it too seriously, if I were you."

"You don't have to apologize to me for them, you know," Michael Wireman said sharply. They were his people, after all—not Potter's.

"Of course. I'm sorry, Michael. I do want to thank you for saving me from my own tongue, back there in the cave."

"I didn't think they were being fair. But—" He found himself smiling wryly. "They *are* naturally tense and overwrought."

Potter made a ridiculous, bottled-up noise in the darkness. After a moment, Michael Wireman realized it was the little man's idea of laughter.

"Well," Michael Wireman said, knowing Potter's amusement was his own fault, but wanting to change the subject nevertheless, "tomorrow we start."

"Yes," Potter said, "we do. I hope Hammil's men aren't too sensitive to be trained."

"I do, too," Michael Wireman said.

He lay in the disheartening darkness, puzzling over what had brought him to Earth. He had not questioned his good fortune when Thomas Harmon proposed sending him. He had been vaguely aware that his father had not liked the idea, but had given in at some unspoken pressure from Harmon—given in with a sigh and an expression of defeat that had never quite disappeared from his face again, particularly whenever Michael found him unexpectedly looking at him. But Michael Wireman had been too dazed—too continually surprised to wake up each morning and realize, in a newly refreshed wave of warmth each morning, that he was going to Earth, and was going to fight, and was going to *do* something—in short, that he was going to begin his life—to stop and think.

He could think now. The edge of excitement was gone, scraped off against Hammil's personality and Newsted's touchiness. He could wonder about this gift horse, now.

It seemed to him that it was a good thing he was here. There might not be much he could do, but he could keep an eye on Hammil. If need be—if Hammil deliberately mismanaged things for his own ends—Michael Wireman could serve as a witness against him.

It was surprising to find himself thinking in these terms. Who would have suspected, on Cheiron, that Hammil was unworthy of liberating Earth? Certainly not Michael Wireman. Thomas Harmon? Had Harmon somehow known enough about Hammil to reach that sort of judgement?

It seemed terribly unlikely. More probably, Harmon's experience in life was such that he could sense a suspicious situation, even from four light-years away. But that sort of prescience seemed remarkable to Michael Wireman.

He knew as little as possible about international diplomacy. He would have been the first to admit that he knew very little about anything. He had, indeed, attended schools in Cheiron. But he had always kept it firmly in mind that a Centaurian education was not particularly applicable to a person whose life could reach its fruition only on Earth.

And he knew very few facts about Earth. His mother, of course, had no reason to have remembered historical details or the minutiae of Earth's social structure. He was positive, however, that in listening to her, hour after hour in his early childhood—hearing the old stories of heroic Earthmen; Charlemagne, Caesar, Napoleon, Washington, Theodore Roosevelt, Winston Churchill—he had absorbed an enormous intuitive grasp of his heritage and the grandeur of Earth's past. He was not certain of where, or in what century, Charlemagne had lived and fought. But he knew him to be a man stern in his devotion to right and duty, to the love of his country, and the principles of justice— just as all Earth's great men had been.

Michael Wireman had no hope of being another Charlemagne, of course. He was afraid of dying, for example, and he did not think he had the moral stamina to laugh at physical pain. These prerequisites to any sort of true leadership simply had not been born into him. As a small boy, of course, he had dreamed the usual childhood dreams. But he was older, now, and perfectly aware of the wide difference between the great men his mother described and himself. He had no idea of what he wanted from life—he was perfectly willing to take what it gave him, since, of course he could not expect to deserve the rewards given to men of strong fiber. He was inordinately pleased to learn that he could, at least, carry a rifle in Earth's liberation.

So, although he regretted, sometimes, that his

father had not found time to teach him the outlook of men who moved the world, he considered that this was very properly his own fault for not displaying as a child the same qualities which he could see in his father and the other grown men around him. Now, perhaps, through personal experience, he would acquire a little of that knowledgeable air. And when the liberation came, perhaps he and his father would thus be drawn a little closer to each other.

"It's cold," Isaac Potter said through chattering teeth.

His current train of thought led Michael Wireman to make a daring remark. He had reasoned out the salient fact about Potter almost as soon as he met him, and the urge to display his own acuity finally overcame him. "I thought they grew them tougher than that in the C.S.O. Secret Service," he said.

"Eh? What's that?" Isaac Potter chattered.

"Nothing, my nervous friend. Nothing." Michael Wireman chuckled wisely to himself, but the cold turned it into a shudder.

"Get up."

It was Newsted's voice, and the toe of Newsted's scarred boot digging relentlessly into the small of his back. But Newsted himself was invisible. Stiff and sore, racked by chills and wet through to the skin, Michael Wireman woke up to find himself entombed. A thick gray-white mist, as palpable as a mass of cobweb, was flowing over his face. He thrashed his head from side to side, his responses overtriggered by a foul-tasting lack of sleep. The world was muffled in glutinous fog all around him.

Newsted probed with persistent viciousness. "*Up,* damn you!"

Michael Wireman pushed himself out of his blanket, and his head cleared the top of the ground mist. The sticky white fog was running down the slope two feet thick, sluicing among the tree trunks and covering the underbrush. The shallow bowl of the valley was flat with a filling of the stuff, and it was spilling over the lower rim and pouring down the mountainside as though this entire range, its vegetation grown and nourished in dark secret deeps, had suddenly thrust itself above the surface of a sea of soured milk.

"Where's Potter?" he mumbled, grinding his face into the palms of his hands.

"With Hammil. Come *on!*"

Michael Wireman stared down into the valley with numb fascination. Something fantastic was going on in there.

The bowl was boiling as though a nest of trapped creatures struggled in it, barely out of sight. He saw something break out near the surface, writhing, and suddenly an arm shot out into the clear air, rigidly extended, then plunged back out of sight as it stabbed downward with a knife clutched in its hand.

Now he saw them. All along the valley rim, the fog was bulging and swirling as men crouched through it. The fog muffled every sound. It was literally still as death, and shadows came crawling over the valley rim, pitched downward, and disappeared into combat in the bowl.

Newsted hauled him to his feet. "They're after the guns. I need you. Come on, or I swear I'll kill you where you stand." The man seized his arms and flung him toward the cave. Half-asleep, still not quite able to realize what was happening, Michael Wireman was struck most of all by an impression of Newsted's strength. Then he stumbled over the uneven ground, found his footing, and began to run, with Newsted at his heels like a terrier.

"We'll never hold them," Newsted was cursing. "They're all over us. And I have to be stuck with you!" The man's voice became a hiss.

"You better not do something to get me killed."

That didn't seem to call for any reply. Michael Wireman ran head-down, his arms pumping. His eyes were swimming, and his ears were clogged. It was becoming obvious that this was not so much sleepiness as it was the beginning of a violent fever. Every joint and muscle in his body was aching.

In the valley, men were dying blind, grasping at shadows and strangling phantoms. The precious guns were in danger. Hammil, Potter, and the entire mission might be wiped out before they had even begun. Here and now, Earth's future might go down to misty oblivion, and Michael Wireman might very well have come four light years to die. But, as he ran, Michael Wireman's dominant emotion was a kind of perverse joy. Twenty years of his life were culminating in this moment. Last night's uncertainty could be resolved.

When he reached the cave, he was grinning with anticipation, Potter was rapidly strapping one bundle of assembled weapons to Ladislas's back. Hammil was standing impatiently beside the other bundle. He nudged it toward Newsted with his foot and snapped: "At last! Very well, don't dawdle now—I'll expect you at the base sometime tomorrow."

Newsted answered Hammil with a spiteful glance, but heaved up the bundle and threw it over his wiry back. Holding it in place, he looked over his shoulder. "Strap it on, Wireman—and don't fumble!"

Michael Wireman looked from Newsted to Hammil. "Aren't we going to stay here and fight? We're just going to run away and leave the men behind?"

Hammil was already turning away to follow Ladislas, and didn't bother to answer. Potter hung back momentarily, and looked at Michael Wireman with discomfort. "We're dividing into two parties, and will meet at a rendezvous. The guns, after all . . . the position here is hopeless. . . ."

Newsted cuffed Michael Wireman's ear sharply. *"Buckle this pack!"*

Ladislas was out of sight, and Hammil was a monochrome figure in the mist, crawling over the valley's upper rim. Potter scrambled up after them.

Michael Wireman fastened the pack straps. He picked up Newsted's rifle as well as his own, and they worked their way up the slope wordlessly, breasting the fog.

3

Once they were over the ridge and on the mountain's western face, Newsted stopped, pressed his back against a boulder, and grunted:

"Break. Two minutes." Sweat was running down his face in sheets, and his threadbare shirt was sopping. They were in clear, hot sunshine now, though Michael Wireman felt it only as a prickling sensation on his flushed skin. He dropped to the ground and squatted with his arms pressed tightly to his ribs.

"I'll carry the pack for a while," he said.

Newsted sneered at him. "You start too slow. If somebody came over that ridge, you'd want to sit and have lunch."

Michael Wireman was perfectly aware of how long he'd fumbled about this morning. He didn't need Newsted to remind him. "We got away from them in the fog. Nobody's going to follow us."

"You think so, eh? And you're sure nobody's waiting down on that slope below." Newsted pushed himself erect. "Let's get crackling. We've got a long way to go. Down this mountain and up the next." The short rest had restored Newsted amazingly. Looking at him as he began scrambling down the slope, balancing the bulky pack as if it were part of his body, Michael Wireman realized that Newsted could go on like this indefinitely—that it would take a man every bit as tough to ever run him down.

This was a species of endurance that Michael Wireman for all his C.S.O. training instructors, had never dreamed existed. It gave him hope for Earth's future. An army of men like Newsted, adequately armed without dependence on stolen Invader weapons and homemade knives, would be a force for any world's infantry to reckon with. Supplemented by trained corps of armor and artillery, supported from the air, and with their opponent's resources localized by the presence of C.S.O. ships in the Solar System, such an army could destroy the Invader garrison on Earth without the C.S.O. landing so much as a single man to help them. From the C.S.O. point of view, it would be an ideal way to fight a war. Cheap in men, and not prohibitive in material. A clean, modern campaign, while Earth's men enjoyed the opportunity to do their vengeful dirty work on the ground.

It would work, Michael Wireman thought. It would *really* work.

He had never doubted it, of course, but now that he actually saw how it might come about he realized that perhaps he had not been as sure as all that. Newsted—saturnine, unlikeable Newsted—had replenished his faith.

That brought his thoughts to Hammil, for whom he had nothing but growing contempt, but before he could dwell on the man very much they were back below the timber line, and Newsted had his arm in one steely hand.

"Now, look, Wireman," Newsted said coldly, "from here on it's going to be tough. Up in the rocks, the chances were fair of even you seeing something before it hit us. Down here in the woods, you haven't got a prayer. Just the same, we need you to do the instructing if Potter doesn't make it, so do me a favor and don't get killed. Watch me. Step where I step. Walk slow or fast according to what I did when I was where you are. Don't talk, don't belch, don't scratch yourself. Never move suddenly. Keep your mouth open wide, but don't use it for anything but breathing. Turn your head from side to side and listen. Smell the breeze. Listen for sounds, but listen harder for silences. Every five paces, look up at the trees. *Remember* that—it's against human nature to look up above eye level for any length of time, but *do* it. Never step out of my trail—not so much as six inches.

"And *watch* me. Watch my ears—they'll twitch if I hear something, and I'm not kidding. If I freeze, you freeze. Watch my hands. If I motion, you do what I signal, and *fast*, but remember to start slow. Whatever happens, don't try and crawl over to me, no matter how quiet you think you can be. Don't ever, no matter what, say a word to me. If we get shot at, don't shoot back until you're sure they know *exactly* where you are. Wait 'til they're just barely missing you. If you see them coming close to me, but ignoring or missing you, that's my tough nut. Don't try and join in." Newsted's eyes glittered, and Michael Wireman had no trouble understanding that the reverse situation was far more likely to apply.

"O.K.," Newsted said, "—think you can remember all that?"

"Yes."

Newsted licked his front teeth. "Yeah." He took his rifle, turned away and began to move downward through the trees, shifting his weight with almost effeminate grace, flowing through the patterns of a ballet that let him approach but never touch either the brush or the trees, and that seemed to permit his feet never to quite press against the ground. Doing his best, Michael Wireman followed. Compared to Newsted, it was a clumsy best. But, in spite of the persistent chills that now were shivering him in regular waves and made optimism difficult, it was a good enough performance to flatter his pride a little. No doubt it would have been laughable to an objective observer, with its awkward twists and near-scrapes. Michael Wireman was sure he resembled a performing bear following Pavlova across stage. But it served the purpose. He began to feel that he might very well, in time, come to take a full place in the armies of free Earth. He wondered how he would react under fire.

*   *   *

Two hours later, they were in a grove of towering pines whose trunks grew straight out of a flat floor thick with slippery needles. There was no brush, no cover of any kind except the trunks themselves, and those were bare of branches for yards over their heads, and well separated. Michael Wireman, following Newsted at a distance of about twenty feet, could see the **man** step out gingerly after a long wait. Newsted was clearly nervous, holding his battered Invader rifle at high port and swinging his body from side to side on his hips as he squinted all around him in the dimly lit grove.

It came home to Michael Wireman that he had been listening to a silence. Far away, a woodpecker's bill went *rattatata!* against a pine trunk, and Michael Wireman did not mistake it for gunfire. But there were no sounds of any kind from anywhere nearer.

Newsted's open hand, palm back, made an inconspicuous stop signal at his side. Then he moved slowly forward, while Michael Wireman froze into position.

The shot, when it came, was nothing like the sound a rifle makes on an open range. It was a dull, sodden boom of almost primitive violence. It flung Newsted's left arm back into the air, threw him to the ground, and shivered the pine it struck in its continued flight. Newsted lay twitching on the ground for a moment, shook his head violently, and reached the nearest tree in one convulsed leap that took Michael Wireman completely by surprise. Newsted rested the barrel of his rifle in the crook of his left elbow, used his right hand to jam his folded left arm securely between his chest and the tree trunk, and, using that for a rest, squatted on his heels and brought his rifle's butt up to his right shoulder again. It was a piece of bulldog stubbornness that thoroughly underscored Michael Wireman's earlier judgement of him as a fighting man. But, as a fighting man, he must have been even more aware than Michael Wireman that he was helpless if forced to shift position.

It grew quiet again. Michael Wireman had not moved. He stayed exactly where he was, half-crouched, his C.S.O. rifle ready but targetless. He could see nothing but the brush immediately in front of him, the open grove a little below him, and Newsted huddled against his tree.

He lined up the shot's path from the tree where it had lodged, through the point Newsted's upper arm had occupied, and back among the ranks of pine. He saw no place likelier than another to be hiding the source of the shot. But he *had* established a line, heading diagonally to his right. He was fairly sure no one along it could see him or had seen him. It seemed likely that if he made a circling cast to his right, he might come up behind anyone within reasonable shooting distance.

If anything new had happened in the grove, he probably would have stayed where he was. But there was no further shooting, and no movement. It seemed likely that there were not enough men down there to disregard even one wounded man's opposition.

That thought made sense to Michael Wireman. A stronger force would have scouted both of them out, surrounded them, and fired from several places at once. A stronger force would now be advancing openly, drawing Newsted's fire and attention from one side to the other in a sort of lethal tennis game. None of these things had happened or, from all indications, were about to.

Ratata! from the distant woodpecker again. A pool of blood was collecting around Newsted's left foot and sending inquisitive rivulets across the glossy brown needles. An invitingly open gap between two bushes to his right beckoned to Michael Wireman. He opened his mouth wide, eased in a silent breath, and took the first necessary step.

That done, it was easier. He moved with the exaggerated caution born of self-aware amateurishness, bent almost double in his care to place his feet. He hoped he was following a consistent line of direction. He stopped often to look to his left and see whether he was in sight of anyone. He knew that if he was wrong—if there were many men placed among the trees—he was dead. But if he stopped now and either went back or stayed where he was, in either case presumably to starve to death while he stayed rooted to the ground, he would be doing the absurd. Years of exposing himself as an ardent Terrestrial patriot to uncaring Centaurian schoolmates had made him sensitive to the commission of ridiculous, and so he went on, nervousness and anticipation growing in him until he would have panted if Newsted's orders had let him.

The slow pace, the care, the tension, the anticipation of combat, all worked against each other in him. The action, when it came, would be an eruption of gunfire and violent motion. His mind raced ahead of his sluggish body, trying to drag him after it. He seethed with the mounting frustration of having to creep, crawl, tiptoe slowly forward.

He came upon them suddenly. Two men crouched

behind trees, staring at the immobile edge of Newsted's pack as it peeped from behind his tree. At the same moment, one of them heard him. Michael Wireman distinctly saw the hair prickle on the nape of his neck. The man gave a strangled cry and rolled aside without ever having looked at what he'd heard.

If the man hadn't swung up his rifle, he might have lived. Michael Wireman's fist closed on the C.S.O. rifle's stock, and his trigger finger jerked convulsively. He sprayed his fire across both trees, both men, and the ground between them, watching the pine needles explode into the air and the slugs punching the fabric of the men's clothes into their bodies.

After a moment, Newsted found him looking down at them. They were ragged, bearded men with grimy skin. He looked at Michael Wireman and snorted a quiet laugh through his nostrils. "What did you think we were running from?" he asked. " 'Vaders?"

"Yes," Michael Wireman answered, "I had thought so."

4

In the dusk, Michael Wireman crouched beside the narrow brook in the valley between the two mountains. His back muscles would not have let him straighten if he wanted to. The pack lay on the ground beside him, where he had let it tumble, and his blanket was wrapped around him in a futile attempt to stop his shivering. There was a faint but maddeningly persistent ringing in his head. Each time he swallowed, his ears popped viciously. All his joints were watery, and the hot, clinging perspiration, for all his chills, would not stop forming on his face.

Newsted, sitting on the bank and re-tying his sling with his right hand and his teeth, glanced at him sidelong. "Look," he said, "the 'Vaders never come up into these mountains. They'd be fools if they did. Nobody in military history has showed much profit fighting irregular troops over broken ground."

"That's very interesting," Michael Wireman muttered thickly.

Newsted seemed plagued by a desire to talk. Perhaps he felt obligated. His manner had not changed dramatically—the sneer was still in his voice, together with tolerant amusement at Michael Wireman's naïveté—but he *was* condescending to explain something, instead of giving orders. His awkwardness at this sort of thing was plain. He groped toward his objective. Michael Wireman noticed and enjoyed it, to his limited capacity at the moment, but there was still dirt under his fingernails that had gotten there when he scooped out a grave, buried the two men, and concealed the fresh earth.

"The 'Vaders don't have any particular reason for coming up here," Newsted went on. "We've never represented any kind of a threat to them. As a matter of fact, they'd probably rather see us up here, out of the way, than down in the towns causing trouble individually. Nobody likes grumblers in his district. Malcontents stir things up; they do damage just by being mule-headed; they keep the jail full. And through it all, they still have to be fed and taken care of. So the 'Vaders leave us alone . . . and . . . we pretty much leave them alone."

"Leaving you plenty of time to fight among yourselves."

"Most of the time, there's the problem of eating," Newsted replied with quick asperity.

"And how do you solve that?"

Newsted clicked his tongue. "Well, you might say the farmers on the slopes around here pay two sets of taxes."

With sundown, the air had grown bitter cold again. Michael Wireman's blanket was little help. He was swaying, rocking back and forth on his heels and toes.

"Can we make a small fire?" he asked.

"You can if you want to die."

A cold chuckle jumped involuntarily out of Michael Wireman's throat.

"We can hole up somewhere around here, though," Newsted said, "and grab some sleep. We only have to get to the top of the next mountain tomorrow. That's definitely Hammil's territory. We'll both have a chance to get warm then."

"Hammil," Michael Wireman said with a twitch of his face.

Newsted made a noise that was half a laugh. "Hammil's a clown. If he didn't have me and Ladislas, he couldn't find his tail with both hands. I told him we bumped into that stranger last night. You know what he said? He said nobody'd dare attack now that he had the guns. Just like that. What in God's world did he think would *make* them attack? What made him think nobody'd realize he couldn't have brought ammunition with him? Everybody knows Hammil. He'll set a rendezvous twenty miles away from his base because he doesn't want to tip its location. But he leaves the ammunition home because it's hard to come by and he doesn't want to risk losing it. Then he goes and loses the men who were going to carry the guns, so the two of us have to wrestle with one bundle while Ladislas takes the other. I get shot. And what's it all for? There's still nine hundred guns to be delivered, and they'll have to be dropped on the base. But Hammil won't feel so bad about that because he'll have a hundred guns ready on the ground in the case that 'Vaders do decide it's worth it to bomb us. A hundred rifles against airplanes!"

Newsted spat on the ground. "You know what those guns are doing to Hammil?" he said. "They're the biggest thing that ever happened to him, so naturally he's running around like a chicken with its head cut off. This is his big chance. Now he gets to strut and be king of the hill, and wave that God-damned commission around. Every dream he's ever had in front of a mirror is coming true. Do you expect him to act like a sensible man?" Newsted had worked himself up into a pitch of surly temper quite unlike his usual sharp irritability. Plainly he was sulking over an old sore.

Curious, Michael Wireman toed the bundle of guns and said: "If that's how you feel, I don't see what's keeping you from taking these guns somewhere else and starting your own organization."

"I could," Newsted said bitterly. "Knock over a 'Vader command post, or something, and get plenty of ammunition. With fifty guns and some good men to go with them, I could carve out quite a piece of these mountains for myself. But, then what? When the guns wear out, so do I." Newsted was no longer bothering to conceal his facial ex-

pressions. Even in the dim light, it was possible to
see all the pent-up envy, all the malice, naked and
blazing.

"Hammil only did two smart things in his life.
The second one was getting hold of that radio and
contacting your people. The first one was something he did by accident thirty years ago. He was a
flat, hopeless failure at everything he tried. The
only thing for him to do was find a place at the
public trough. So he got himself that miserable
reserve Lieutenant's commission. And look what
it's brought him.

"What would have happened if it had been me
that got the radio? If I called up and said: 'Hey,
this is Joe Newsted. I'd like to go out and liberate
Earth. Drop me some guns.' A C.S.O. secret agent
would have prowled through the old Earth Government records the 'Vaders had piled up somewhere, and he would have found my old police
dossier, that's what, just like he found Hammil's
old army dossier. And I could have whistled for
my guns. But Hammil—Hammil, now, that never
budged when the 'Vaders came, that surrendered
his platoon without firing a shot—*he* gets his thousand guns, and more besides." Newsted was actually pouting. "It could have been almost anybody.
That's the part that burns me the worst. Anybody
at all, as long as he had the pipeline to the guns.
Once he got the guns, it made no difference if he
had a hundred men, a thousand, ten, or none at
all. He'll have 'em now. No matter how much they
hate Hammil, they know which side their bread is
buttered on. And nobody's going to do anything
about him. He's your official boy—he's got a mo-
nopoly, now, and a loyal army to protect it."
Newsted's face twisted. "He's a baboon—a hairy,

posturing baboon. He's got only one thing, when you come right down to it—he's stupid enough to believe in his own poses. He really thinks he's a man of destiny—a great leader of men. He believes it, and, by God, sometimes it gets so thick you can't help believing in it yourself.

"That's the difference between us. If I struck attitudes like his, I couldn't do it with a straight face. He can. I'm smarter than he is—hell, almost anybody's smarter than he is!—and that's why I have to play second fiddle to a baboon."

Staggering under his load, listening to Newsted curse with pain behind him, Michael Wireman somehow reached Hammil's base on the next mountain. Far below him, on the horizon, a city lay in geometrical exactitude. Here on the mountainside, clumsily built cabins and leanto's shambled under the trees, wrapped in the stench of a camp that had been too long in one place. Dirty, ragged men came to meet them. Flies attacked him immediately.

Michael Wireman pitched forward, unconscious.

5

"He's better, I see." Hammil's voice was crisp. He stood in a decisive pose, hands on his hips, a riding crop tucked into the top of one boot. Michael Wireman leaned his back into the corner of his bunk, drew up his knees, and went on drinking soup out of the canteen top held in his cupped hands.

Isaac Potter looked up from the chair where he

had been sitting and carefully pulling the slugs out of stolen Invader cartridges. "Yes, he is."

"Two days," Hammil commented. "He recovered fast."

It had taken practically all the antibiotics in Potter's and Michael Wireman's medical kits, but he had recovered, in a manner of speaking. The fever was gone. It had been replaced by a warm weak stupor, a reactive skin rash which he often found himself scratching absently, and a feeling of utter detachment. He studied Hammil with mild curiosity.

"Well, he's a young man," Potter said to Hammil in his habitually high-pitched voice. He seemed to find it necessary to lock eyes with Hammil. "It wouldn't be so easy for him to die of natural causes."

That made Hammil blink. He plucked the riding crop out of his boot and slapped fitfully at his calf with it. "I'm not certain of your meaning." He shifted his eyes for a quick glance at Michael Wireman, then twitched them back. He made a frown at Potter. "Are you saying I would try to have the boy murdered?" Even counting the frown, he seemed singularly unindignant.

"No," Potter said, shaking his head seriously. "I really would not think so. But sometimes people may wish that luck will accomplish something for them that they themselves would not quite undertake."

Hammil blinked again. He rapped his boot viciously with the riding crop. He half-turned. "I came in to see about the boy's health. I see he's well, I'm satisfied." He completed his turn and marched out of the cabin.

Michael Wireman finished his soup.

After a while, he lay down again, his hands cupped behind his head. "Potter?"

"Yes, Michael?"

"Did the ship drop the rest of the guns?"

"Last night."

"You thought it was all right to give them to Hammil, in spite of everything?"

There was a short pause from Potter. "Yes," he said after that moment. "I did."

"Do you like Hammil?"

"No."

"I'm glad I don't have your assignment."

"Why, Michael?"

"Well, I'm here. I'm committed. My decisions were all made back on Centaurus—made by me or for me, I'm not sure which—and even if I wanted to change them now, I can't. But you're the one who's not only in the middle of something unexpected, but also has to make decisions accordingly. When they gave you your orders on Centaurus, they didn't expect Hammil's wonderful army to be what it is. It looked pretty cut and dried. Supply the man with arms, let him start something going, and then bring in support. But now it turns out that if ever a single Invader is going to die by those guns, you're going to have to do a massive job of persuasion. Hammil won't move. He'll terrorize the other bands in these mountains, and become king of the brigands, but he'd die of heart failure if he had to move against the Invaders."

There was another pause from Potter. Then he said gently: "You're wrong, Michael. I have no decisions to make. Perhaps you do, but I don't. I only have to let things roll downhill exactly as they're doing. Hammil will move against the Invaders."

"Hammil couldn't find his tail with both hands if he didn't have Newsted," Michael Wireman answered with his first show of emotion.

"But he has Newsted," Potter said. "And Ladislas. They'll push him into it."

"Why should they?"

"Because . . ." Potter sighed, "because they want to rule the world. They think that once Hammil has driven out the Invaders, he will become the military dictator of Earth. Hammil thinks so, too. But Newsted and Ladislas, together or separately, expect to rule Hammil. And that is why Hammil, who is a blustering coward, will march against the Invaders. That is why Newsted, who is a thief, will encourage him. That is why Ladislas, who was a professor of political science in the old days and is much more fluent in languages other than English, is content to carry seventy-five pound bundles up mountainsides and polish Hammil's boots. And that is why you, no matter how good a fighting man you become, will never be accepted by these men."

Michael Wireman had nothing to say. Isaac Potter went back to work with his pliers. Flies buzzed about inside the cabin. It was a full hour before Michael Wireman rolled over on his side, picked the canteen top up from the floor beside his bunk, and held it out. "Would you get me some more soup, please?" he said.

Isaac Potter nodded, took the cup, and went inside to the fire. He came back and handed it to him.

"You know," Michael Wireman said in a distant voice, "when I was a boy, I spent most of my time with my mother. She told me stories about what Earth was like—about the kind of people Earthmen were. And looking back at what I could see of the people on the ship with us, it was all true. People were friendly, polite—good. Good people. Everyone was always very nice to me." He sipped at the warm cup. "Of course, my mother was the President's wife, and I was the President's son. As I grew older, I thought about that. But I didn't think very hard. Why should I? It was too nice a thing for me to scratch holes in it. But I'm twenty-five, now, and I'm here." He took another swallow. "You're all right, Potter. You're doing your job. And when you come right down to it, Hammil and the rest can't be blamed. They're far away from the Government in Exile. They've had a tough time of it. They're the kind of men they are, so they'd naturally ignore the old Government. And presumably it makes no difference to the C.S.O. what kind of Earthmen run this world, as long as the Invaders get pushed out.

"I guess," he said, finishing the soup and putting the cup down, "I'm the only one here who ought to care one way or the other. But right now, I don't think I care very much." He rolled over and, after a little while, fell into a kind of sleep.

In the three days that followed, Michael Wireman got back on his feet again, and even managed to help Potter with instructing the men. It was a fairly simple job. Whatever they had been before, the older men had learned weapons very well in the past years. The younger ones had grown up with rifles. They had to be taught not to hold the trigger down, and to allow for the weapon's tendency to buck up and to the left, and that was about all. They learned quickly. Hammil watched their progress impatiently, but even he couldn't complain. Michael Wireman talked to almost no one, except in line of duty, and when he did he talked in monosyllables. He had decided it was best that way, and nothing happened to prove him wrong.

6

"You men," Hammil said, posed in front of the fire, silhouetted in his widespread stance, "you men are my staff." He tasted the words. "My staff."

Newsted and Ladislas were lying on the ground, Ladislas looking impassively up at the stars, and Newsted in a careless sprawl. Potter sat upright on a boulder, his eyes bright and curious. Hammil had called them all away from the rest of the men, his whole manner fraught with the anticipation of triumph. Now he was being the military genius.

Michael Wireman, who had followed inconspicuously along behind Potter, felt his lip curling. He squatted in the shadows behind the plump little Centaurian, and watched silently.

"Get to it, Franz," Newsted said wearily.

Hammil glared at him. Newsted laughed: "And can the dramatics. What's up?"

Not even Newsted could put Hammil off tonight. He had been excited ever since one of his scouts had come toiling up the mountain late in the afternoon and given him some sort of private report. Now he was ready to enlighten the others.

"I've decided to initiate the first step in our plan of attack against the Invaders," he said grandly, one eye on Potter.

"If you mean we're gonna go down and knock

off that 'Vader command post along the highway, why don't you say so and get it over with?" Newsted was giving Hammil no scope for grandiose exhibitions. Ladislas grunted softly from where he lay, his lumpy face impassive.

"I'll thank you to show some courtesy, Newsted!" Hammil snapped.

"Shove it," Newsted answered casually. "You're a bag of gas anyhow. Maybe you'd make a bigger noise that way."

"Gentlemen," Potter piped up, "I'm delighted to see that General Hammil has been able to prepare a plan on such short order. This is very encouraging."

"We goin' tomorrow?" Ladislas rumbled.

Whatever might have happened between Hammil and Newsted was now diverted by Hammil's having to pay attention to two people at the same time. Michael Wireman doubted if anything serious would have happened in any case. Newsted's bitterness would need periodical outlets—this sort of bickering was probably the usual thing in this camp. Once again Michael Wireman found new reasons for the bleak lethargy that had crept over him. If these were his people, then it was time to choose another. Perhaps it was time to grow up and admit that twenty years of living on Cheiron was a better heritage than the fact of having been born on a world that was nothing like his false conception of it.

He searched hard for, and found, an actual trace of homesickness for Cheiron and the C.S.O.

Hammil had recovered his pose. "Very well, then—we're agreed. Tomorrow morning I'll lead a combat patrol against the Invader command post."

You'll lead it? Michael Wireman thought. He'd

hardly expected Hammil to do anything but send Ladislas or Newsted in his place. "I want to go along," he spoke up.

Hammil peered into the shadows. "What're you doing here?"

"Nobody said anything about my staying with the rank-and-file," Michael Wireman answered. "So I tagged along. What's the odds—do you think I'm going to peddle your military secrets to the enemy? Do I come along? I want to see you under fire, Hammil. Just once, I'd like to see that."

Hammil's eyes narrowed. Then he smiled unpleasantly. "You're more than welcome, Wireman."

"Thanks." Michael Wireman found himself enjoying the feeling of this careless disrespect. It gave him a feeling of being hard, and dangerous, and as mature as any of them, to face Hammil down. "And I *won't* get myself killed. I wouldn't do you that favor." He lapsed back into silence, not even looking at Hammil anymore. He hardly cared how any of them reacted. Potter sighed quietly.

As it finally formed up, the raiding party consisted of ten men, plus Hammil, Ladislas, Potter, and Michael Wireman. Newsted stayed behind to command the camp, with a hard-eyed personal guard of Hammil's ready to assassinate him if he tried to subvert the men.

Hammil was a flushed, excited figure as they worked their way down the mountain slope toward the highway that wound around its foot. In the clear morning sunlight, his head was up and his nostrils were flared. From time to time he smiled to himself with a terrible satisfaction, and he scrambled downward at an impatient pace. Clearly, he had forgotten any possibilities of interception by members of rival bands. Or perhaps he felt that on this day of obvious destiny, no ill chance could keep him from his objective.

"Look at him," Michael Wireman said to Potter as they followed him. "I never thought I'd see him quite so eager."

Ladislas, who was striding on Potter's other side, grunted. "He wants that command post bad. He's wanted it for a long time."

Potter nodded. "I've heard something about that."

"So this is a private raid of some kind," Michael Wireman said.

Potter shrugged. "It makes no difference to me, as long as I have a chance to see how these people handle themselves against Invaders."

"I don't care, either," Michael Wireman said.

Farther down the mountain's slope, it grew hot and humid. The party walked a little more slowly, now. Even Hammil seemed conscious of the fact that his tunic was dark with perspiration. The trees grew thickly, their bases choked by underbrush and fallen leaves. Michael Wireman heard a faint *ratatat* and smiled grimly.

Abruptly Ladislas moved forward, touched Hammil's shoulder, and reminded him of something. Hammil nodded, and swung the party off to the left, taking them no further down the mountain. Ladislas dropped back and fell in beside Michael Wireman. "Now we're going parallel to the highway, until we get above the cross roads where the command post is." He did not comment that Hammil would have led them straight down and probably along the open road if he had not intervened.

"How's your father, boy?" he asked abruptly.

"He was well when I left him," Michael Wireman answered. "Why—did you know him?"

"I ran against him in the last elections." It had apparently been important to Ladislas to tell him that. Now that he'd done so, he relapsed into silence.

"What Professor Danko did not tell you," Potter said, "was that he only lost by fifteen electoral votes."

Michael Wireman looked at the striding giant. He was burned brown and tough. His jaw had no sag of flesh beneath it. His eyes, which Michael Wireman realized he should have paid more attention to, were clear, vivid green. He had to be at least fifty-five. He looked forty.

One of Michael Wireman's strongest memories was of his father, dressed in his cheap trousers, bent forward peering, and picking at the apartment wall with a table knife and a saucerful of crack patching compound. The saucer had dripped on the rug, and the compound had left matted circles.

"Lost, eh?" Michael Wireman said, looking at Ladislas Danko. "I wish you'd won."

The command post was a simple concrete blockhouse on the T-shaped intersection of two roads. It was set in a cleared area at the head of the T, and was obviously there to keep back mountaineer ambitions, nothing more. The blockhouse was painted white, with a flowering border around it trimmed off by precise rows of white painted stones. A walk from the front door to the highway was divided to pass around a circular rock garden from whose center rose a white metal flagpole. An Invader flag licked restlessly back and forth in the warm breeze. There was a stovepipe coming out of the roof, in a corner where a kitchen would be, and the cleared area had been carefully planted in grass, rolled, no doubt watered faithfully, and turned into a lawn with clipped edges. There was an unarmored sedan parked in a drive beside the blockhouse, and an enameled steel signboard read: "Pennsylvania State Police." It was altogether a typical military installation in times of absolute peace, and Michael Wireman could picture a Master Sergeant, or some equivalent, worrying more about the condition of the lawn than he did about the readiness of his guns.

Hammil and Ladislas together spread the party out into a semicircle whose wings fell just short of the main highway. The blockhouse was cupped in the semicircle, but well inside its clearing.

The prospect of crossing that open ground seemed to have no effect on Hammil. Perhaps he did not include cowardice among his failings, after all, or perhaps he really wanted that blockhouse very badly. He stood upright for a moment, only a few yards inside the brush, and looked about him at his men. He nodded to Ladislas, who put two fingers in his mouth and whistled piercingly. Along with the rest of the party, Michael Wireman trotted forward. Potter, beside him, had a tense little half-smile on his face. Michael Wireman was wooden-faced.

They burst out of the brush and threw themselves flat at its edge, firing precisely. Conical bits of the blockhouse wall disappeared, as though a malicious invisible boy had run along them striking with a ball-peen hammer at the level of the window slits.

It was a cold shock to Michael Wireman, how

quickly the light automatic cannon popped their
muzzles through those slits and began firing back.
He stared in amazement at the methodical series
of orange flashes that stuttered in their muzzles.

The Invader fire swept into the men on the side
opposite Michael Wireman, and ploughed up the
ground among them. They were dispersed, and
hard to hit, but even so some of them did not live
through it. There was a *crump!*, and a rusty flower
of smoke broke out near them. So one of Hammil's
demolitions men was gone, his hand-made bomb
with him.

For one moment, it was obvious that they could
never win. Then fire from the C.S.O. weapons
poured into the firing slits, and no gunner could
have kept aim or head against that volume. The
Invader guns began shooting sporadically and wildly.
Another one of Hammil's demolitions men jumped
to his feet, ran erratically forward, swung his arm,
and flung the stuffed canvas bag of Invader rifle
powder against the blockhouse wall. Simultaneously,
the fuse reached the primer, there was a noise like
an oil drum being punched open, and a gap two
feet across crumbled out of the wall. Hammil
screamed out: "Charge!" as though he commanded
cavalry, and then they were all running forward,
covered by the blank in the command post's defenses. They flung themselves desperately through
the gap, losing two more men to small arms fire,
but they took the blockhouse with no further trouble. Michael Wireman sat down with his back to a
wall, and reloaded his rifle.

What must have been a neat interior was now as
dusty as though the blockhouse had been abandoned for years. Even the dead Invader trooper
lying a few feet away—it was impossible to believe

he had ever been capable of life. There was too
much dust on him.

Small-caliber shell cases littered the floor. One
of them, touching Michael Wireman's leg, was
hot. The walls were ripped and cracked, and it
was easy to think of the invisible boy again, smash-
ing out wildly at the embodiments of authority.

Hammil came back into the room through an
inner door. He was grinning mercilessly, and prodding an Invader officer ahead of him with the butt
of his riding crop. Michael Wireman looked at
them curiously.

The Invader was tall and lanky, with sunken
cheeks, prominent cheekbones and a scimitar nose.
He had skin the color of sand, crisp, curly brown
hair, brown eyes, and a long jaw. Someone had
once remarked, in a foolish attempt at the only
Invader joke on record, that Earth had been con-
quered by a race of trackmen. Someone else had
replied that they seemed to win their events, and
that had closed the subject. The Invader officer,
with his severe, functional uniform and his un-
bending height, looked typical of his people. He
walked fast enough to escape most of the force of
Hammil's prodding, without once giving the impression that he was flinching away from it, and,
once in the room, he stopped, turned, and stood
erect, his hands at his sides. He had to bend his
neck down a little to look directly at Hammil, and
that did nothing to detract from the impression he
made.

His eyes flicked once, not over Michael Wireman but over the weapon in his hands, and his lips
compressed just a little. Except for that, he kept
his eyes on Hammil.

Hammil, hands on hips, grinned up at him. "Do

you know me?" he barked in a voice shrill with excitement.

"You're Franz Hammil," the Invader said calmly. "I remember you."

Hammil's grin widened. "And where do you remember me from?"

"I supervised your classification test groups, eight years ago."

"And you thought you'd never see me again."

"It was a matter of indifference to me."

With a vicious twist of his arm, Hammil cut the Invader across the face with his riding crop. The Invader seemed to have been expecting it. His head did not jerk back, and he ignored the open gash on his cheek.

Probably because they'd heard the sound, Potter and Ladislas came quietly into the room and stopped beside Michael Wireman, who suddenly found himself on his feet. "What's going on?" Potter whispered.

"Something about a classification test. I don't know." Now Michael Wireman found himself trembling with rage, and he looked at himself in surprise.

"Oh." It was Ladislas. "He's found his man."

Both Hammil and the Invader ignored everything but each other. Hammil probably had his ears full of the sound of his surging pulse. The Invader might have noticed them—it was hard to believe there was anything he might not notice—but he gave no sign of it.

"You supervised my classification test," Hammil was shrilling. "You supervised it. A boy fresh out of your military college then, and not much more than that now. You supervised classification tests

on former Terrestrial military officers with twice—
ten times—your experience!"

"I did. I remember you were found totally unfit
for command."

No one was surprised when Hammil struck the
Invader again. The new gash overlaid the old.
Thick, venous blood seeped down the Invader's
jaw and dripped from his chin. It dirtied his blouse,
and he paid absolutely no attention to it.

"You did. You did, and do you still hold that
opinion?"

"Classification test scores are not open to opinion. But I will say you've proved them right."

Hammil struck him again, and simultaneously
Ladislas felt it necessary to take the rifle out of
Michael Wireman's hand.

"You didn't think I knew where you were, did
you? You thought you were safe!"

"I knew where you were. I saw no reason why
the reverse might not be true."

Perhaps Hammil began to realize that the Invader was coldly egging him on. Instead of hitting
him, he glared up. "Are you laughing at me?"

"A little."

A shudder swept over Hammil's body, and his
entire skull turned beet red. He screwed up his
face and kicked the Invader viciously in the shins.
"*Hang him from the flagpole!*" His voice whistled
through his constricted throat and emerged as a
venomous piping.

Ladislas moved forward, shouldering Michael
Wireman back, and the dangerous moment was
over. He took the Invader officer by the arm and
led him outside. The Invader walked slowly and
steadily along the gravelled path until they came
to the flowering circle. One of Hammil's men pulled

the flag down on its halliards which were made of tough metal-stranded rope.

The Invader officer's eyes were perhaps a little softer than they had been. But he never spoke.

7

They had dug the six graves and buried their casualties. Hammil had insisted on leaving the dead Invader personnel where they lay—one way or another, not a man in the command post had survived—so now they had nothing left to do. The dismounted Invader cannon, together with as much ammunition as could be found, had been loaded on the backs of men detailed to carry them.

Nevertheless, the party did not pull back immediately. Hammil was standing by himself, looking down at the ground and slapping his boot absently. Some driving purpose had gone out of him. The raid on the blockhouse was over, but Hammil seemed to be having difficulty in bringing himself to realize it.

"What about those classification tests?" Michael Wireman asked Ladislas. "What are they?" There was a definite nauseated taste in his throat, and he pushed words past it in an attempt to force it back down.

Potter answered the question. "It's part of the Invader administrative system to test everyone for aptitude. The population is then classified, and its individual members are assigned to the duties they can best perform. A man on the job he does best can't help but be pleased with himself. A pleased population is not a rebellious one. Hammil requested a test for military aptitude—it was his

option, under Invader law, to try for what he
thought he could do. You know what the result
was. It's all in the file we have on him."

"I see. He tried to become an officer in the
Invader army."

"And was classified out," Ladislas said. "He ran
away into the mountains. I don't think they tried
hard to stop him. They're a funny people. If you
don't fit into their system, they don't force you.
They simply let you starve to death from your own
incompetence. They're not very perturbed if you
run away to someplace harmless."

"That's very interesting," Michael Wireman said.

There was a golden gnat buzzing in the sky.
Michael Wireman looked up. Plane, he thought,
and wondered if the Invaders had some means of
closely observing the ground from that altitude.

Then one moment the plane was nothing but a
sparkling dot against a cloud, and the next it was
among them. Golden, javelin-shaped, the air around
it boiling with the leakage from the modified
spacedrive that powered it, shrieking, wrapped
in its plume of foaming violent air, the Invader
plane tore at them in its beauty.

They ran in all directions, some of them into the
woods, and safety, and some of them into the
blockhouse, whose roof exploded under a shower
of missiles. Michael Wireman, crouching in the
brush, saw a line of rockets march across the lawn,
stand for an instant like tubular fence posts, and
explode their warheads in sequence. Or perhaps it
was just that his mind was filtering visual impres-
sions with such rapidity that he was actually able
to separate impact from detonation. A power-driven
antipersonnel missile ought to be fuzed to explode its warhead on proximity, he knew—otherwise

the warhead was already too deep in the ground to do much damage. Perhaps these were armor-piercing missiles, intended for some other target entirely. The spaceship, perhaps. The plane would be on a regular patrol mission, then.

So this was what Invader radar had made of the ship. And it had done well, for though the plane was gone, now, missiles expended, still Isaac Potter crouched over the grass, his hands clasped to his stomach.

Michael Wireman ran toward him, stumbling over the smoky craters in the lawn. He ran fast, but Hammil reached the pudgy little man first, from farther away.

Potter had dropped to his knees. His mouth was a round O, and he had gone white. Hammil pushed him down on his back and pulled his hands away from his body. He looked, turned him over roughly, looked at his back, and turned him back again. Potter stared up at him dumbly.

Michael Wireman shouldered Hammil aside. "Leave him alone! *Leave* him *alone!*"

Hammil paid him absolutely no attention. He was fumbling at the breast pocket of his tunic. He kneaded his fingers frantically, trying to work the button, until finally he tore it off and plunged his hand into the pocket. The first piece of paper he pulled out was his commission. He looked at it impatiently and threw it aside. The next was a folded sheaf of document paper. He opened it on his knee and began searching his pockets for something to write with.

Isaac Potter had put his hands back. He began trying to speak, tensing his neck with the effort. His mouth opened and closed several times. He saw Michael Wireman and tried harder.

"Not secret service," he finally managed. "Department of Exterior Affairs. Diplomatic corps."

Hammil had found a pencil. He turned over the last page in the bundle of document paper, brushed the pencil tip across the end of his tongue, and knelt beside Potter. He braced the document against his thigh and pushed the pencil into Potter's right hand. "Sign it," he said in a panicky voice. "Sign it. You were going to, if the raid was a success."

Potter grimaced with a twitch of his whole body. "Success. Yes. But look out for airplanes in future, eh?" He executed the signature with great care. Then he handed the pencil to Michael Wireman. Something entirely unlike physical pain crossed his features. "You sign it, too. Witness."

Without much caring, Michael Wireman signed the document. Potter handed it back to Hammil. "Go find Ladislas. You need two. Good, reputable witnesses. President's son, President's opposition. Go ahead, man. It's done."

Hammil nodded, his eyes blazing. He stood up, stopped, bent over, and picked up his commission. Putting it back in his pocket, he strode toward the edge of the clearing.

Potter gathered himself. "I don't know what he wants that commission for. But, of course, he couldn't just leave it. That . . . I signed . . . was a treaty. Between the Centaurian System Organization and Franz Hammil, President Pro Tem of Earth. Mutual assistance. He protects us from all attempts to overthrow the rightful government of Centaurus, and we do a like service for him. We've—bypassed your people entirely, Michael. A little too high-minded for us. We can handle Hammil.

"See, we *couldn't* let Earth go back to complete

independence. Too big a risk. We've *got* to have men and bases out here permanently, now."

"Potter. . . ."

"Policy, Michael. Have to plan for a generation ahead. Have to be sure we'll always be free."

And having said that, Isaac Potter died.

Michael Wireman became conscious of Ladislas's hand on his shoulder. "We'll take him with us," the giant rumbled. "Bury him up on the mountain. The 'Vaders'll be coming up with an armored ground patrol any minute."

Michael Wireman looked around. The rest of the party was already gone. Hammil had pulled the men back, leaving Potter to lie where he'd died.

Michael Wireman took one breath, and another. He moved out from under Ladislas's grasp and slipped his rifle off his shoulder. It fell to the ground, its muzzle lying across Potter's ankles. He began walking away, across the lawn, and then he was walking down the highway, toward the oncoming Invaders, his hands raised in the air.

THREE

1

The Invader patrol was at first nothing more than an approaching motor noise behind a dip in the sunbaked asphalt road. Then a small armored gun-carrier jounced over the nearest rise and braked hurriedly at the sight of Michael Wireman standing there. It was already near the middle of the day. It was hot, and Michael Wireman's dirty coveralls were sodden. He kept his arms up despite the throb of the sudden bad headache, and looked expressionlessly at the muzzle of the carrier's machine gun.

An Invader officer, natty and forbidding in his silver-corded black uniform, looked curiously out. "Are you surrendering, boy?"

Michael Wireman nodded.

"Well, for Heaven's sakes get off the roadway! Are you trying to get yourself run down?" He gestured impatiently, and Michael Wireman, with a shrug, stepped backward onto the shoulder. The officer nudged his driver and the gun-carrier slid over to a stop beside him, its exhaust popping down to a murmurous idle.

A column of six armored trucks hurried by with a blast of wind. The officer spoke briefly into a radio microphone, and a duplicate gun-carrier which had been bringing up the rear of the column suddenly put on a burst of speed, passed the trucks, and took up the lead position. The patrol disappeared in the direction of the gutted Invader command post. Michael Wireman and the Invaders were left alone in the road, with the pine woods to either side of them and the flank of the nearest mountain rising up at the north.

The officer swung out a lean leg and rested his boot on the fender. He lounged back in his seat, frowning at Michael Wireman, studying his face and clothes, and finally said, impatiently. "You can drop your hands, son. Now—what's all this about?"

Michael Wireman clasped his hands behind his back. "I'm surrendering."

"I can see that. But, why?" It became obvious he was genuinely non-plussed. Like ninety-nine out of a hundred of the Invaders now on Earth, he was clearly too young to have served in the war. A member of one naturally gregarious race in the midst of another greatly like it except that the two could not interbreed, he was totally unused to trouble. He knew there were dissidents in the mountains, but he was unused to trouble from them either. He, along with every young officer on Earth, undoubtedly longed for transfer to the frontier in some solar system where things were not so everlastingly routine, even while he enjoyed the agreeable relaxation of garrison duty.

Paradoxically, he was also unused to the thought

of a dissident's surrendering. But there was no paradox about it. Dissidents, after all, properly belonged in their isolated mountains, moving in a world separated from his own. In spite of the fact that he was hurrying to the site of a completely unexpected guerilla attack, it had not quite registered with him that a change had come over his life. He regarded Michael Wireman in the only way he could: as a puzzling, obscurely motivated intruder upon his world.

Belatedly, now as he waited for answer, it occurred to the officer that all this might be a trick. He looked about him at the woods in sudden wariness. Then it became obvious that any trap would have been sprung long ago. Exasperated at finding himself still alive through no credit to himself, he snapped: "Well?"

Michael Wireman could think of no short way to explain the complicated state of his mind. He could not even understand it himself. He had obeyed an impulse, and here he was. "I've had enough," he said in a monotone. "I'm quitting."

"You've killed enough of us and now you want to call time? Is that it?"

Michael Wireman shook his head. "I haven't killed any of you, as far as I know. I was in the attack on the post, I just fired my gun. I might have hit somebody—I don't know. I don't care. I've just plain had enough."

"Open your mouth," the officer said suddenly. "Let me see your teeth." He stared fiercely at Michael Wireman's incomprehension, and said: "Come on! Do it!"

Michael Wireman skinned his lips apart, feeling foolish. The officer reached out suddenly and felt the cloth of his coveralls. He seemed to learn something from all this, and belatedly Michael Wireman realized what it might be. The officer was studying him intently.

"You haven't been in those mountains very long. And that's no terrestrial coverall you're wearing. Where'd you come from?"

Now that it was too late, Michael Wireman still could not bring himself to speak. He simply shook his head, appalled at not having thought how much his surrender might involve. He should have stopped to think, he realized now. But it was too late. He had started a process he was helpless to cut short before it reached its sorry end.

For the first time, Michael Wireman understood exactly what surrender does to a man. He let the breath out of his chest, not caring anymore whether his shoulders slumped or no.

"I'm from Cheiron," he admitted. "I was dropped into the mountains by parachute ten days ago."

"So you're a Centaurian spy."

"I'm a Free Terrestrial," Michael Wireman shot back.

The Invader officer had to think for a minute. Then it came to him.

"Oh ho," he said, leaning back once again. "From the Government in Exile?"

Michael Wireman nodded.

"And you're surrendering." The officer toyed with the channel switch on his radio transmitter. "That's very interesting." He flipped the switch. "Give me Regional Headquarters," he said. "Lieutenant Boros here." He waited, tapping one knee with the fingers of his free hand, and looking steadily at Michael Wireman.

Something had to break the awkward silence.

Michael Wireman blurted: "They hanged the officer in charge on the command post."

Lieutenant Boros' lips disappeared in a pinched,
pale face.

"From the flagpole," Michael Wireman went on
unrelentingly.

"Shut up!"

"I was trying to explain. . . ." Michael Wireman's voice trailed away. He hadn't explained anything. He stared down at his boots.

"Headquarters? Lieutenant Boros, co-commanding
relief patrol to Route 209 command post. I'm bringing in a prisoner." There was a pause. "No, sir.
Lieutenant Laram would have notified me of any
contact with the dissident main body. This was a
stray. Voluntary surrender, and he's willing to talk.
Yes, sir. I'll bring him in right away."

He hung up the microphone, reached around,
and opened the rear door. He got out, unholstered
his sidearm, and squeezed himself into the back
seat. He pointed the sidearm coldly at the vacated
place beside the impassive driver. Lieutenant Boros
was a great deal less of a peacetime soldier now.

"Get in, traitor," he said.

Michael Wireman felt the blood burn in his cheeks.

The route to Regional Headquarters led past the
command post, back the way Michael Wireman
had come.

Two men from the relief patrol were re-hanging
the battered Pennsylvania State Police sign. There
was a short row of shrouded bodies laid out beside
one wall. The Invader flag was back on its pole.
The transport trucks were parked in orderly fashion in the small parking lot behind the post, next
to the burned shell of the police patrol car.

Lieutenant Boros tapped the driver's shoulder. "Stop and blow your horn." The muzzle of his sidearm pressed lightly against the back of Michael Wireman's neck. Inertia pressed it deeper into the flesh as the gun-carrier slowed.

The gun-carrier stopped, and the driver tapped his horn button. The riot siren spun out a brief growl. The officer in charge of the patrol raised his head from where he was kneeling beside one of the bodies, stood up, and came walking over. Like Boros, like the officer Franz Hammil had hanged, he might have been one of a family.

There had to be fat, short, pale Invaders as well, Michael Wireman thought. But it was almost as if some factor in the Invader society had, for a long time now, been selecting for sunken cheeks, aquiline noses, short curly hair and a tall, loose-jointed wiriness. With their dark faces and deep-set brown eyes, they all seemed to be communicants at one flame. It was their very unity that made so sharp a contrast with the terrestrials they resembled. There was this sense of meshing about them—of equal interdependence, equal efficiency, perfect brotherhood.

Well, they had won the war—and this quality of superhuman precision had likely been the vital difference.

The new officer saw Michael Wireman before he saw Lieutenant Boros in the rear compartment. He frowned, and studied Michael Wireman wordlessly, his hand dropping to his sidearm with a smooth, unhurried gesture. There was something genuinely deadly in the way he did it, and Michael Wireman was grateful when Lieutenant Boros said:

"It's all right, Kado," in the compact Invader language.

Kado Laram's face was subtly stiffened by recent shock. Although he had not seen Boros in the back seat before now, he registered no surprise but merely swung his glance without moving his head. Very probably, he was temporarily incapable of thinking in long chains.

"Thon," Laram said quietly, "they got away. They killed everybody here. They seem to have taken no prisoners, and they—"

"Hanged Arl. Yes." Boros' sidearm muzzle poked sharply at Michael Wireman. "He told me."

"Are you taking him to the city?" Laram asked, studying Michael Wireman again.

"Yes."

"Don't lose him."

"I won't."

"Has he told you who was in charge of the dissidents?"

"Franz Hammil," Michael Wireman said.

"Speaks our language," Laram said with some interest but no surprise. He was more interested in the name he'd heard. "Franz Hammil."

"Do you know him?" Michael Wireman asked bitterly.

Laram looked through him, and nodded distantly. "Oh, yes."

There was no need for anyone to enlarge on the point, Michael Wireman thought.

"Tell me, linguist," Laram said in a conversational tone, "did you have anything to do with hanging our friend?"

Michael Wireman shook his head. It seemed unimportant to him whether he was believed or not.

"He's a peculiar one," Lieutenant Boros said. "He's from the old Terrestrial Government in Exile, on Cheiron. They'll want to know, down at Headquarters, just what he was sent to do."

Lieutenant Laram had apparently decided he'd learned enough from his study of Michael Wireman. "He'll tell them," he said. "Whatever it was, they sent a boy on a man's errand."

"I just want to surrender," Michael Wireman said doggedly. "That's all."

"You've been accommodated there, son," Lieutenant Boros said. He turned to Laram. "I'd better get this down to Headquarters. I'll see you back at the barracks."

Laram nodded. "All right." He turned and went back to supervise the careful loading of the bodies into one of the trucks.

Lieutenant Boros tapped the driver's shoulder. "Let's go," he said, and the driver engaged the clutch. The gun-carrier shot out on the highway again, and sped toward the city.

Once out of the foothills, the highway led through dairy country, passing small villages and towns. Everything looked neat and prosperous. There were well-fed, clean people out in the fields and on the town sidewalks. Everything seemed to have a recent coat of paint. There were a number of good-looking civilian vehicles on the road, and the store windows were full of consumer goods. Every so often, someone would wave a friendly hand to the hurrying gun-carrier, and at no time was there a sign of a frown or a half-hidden scowl. Michael Wireman received an overwhelming impression of a contented populace which regarded the gun-carrier as just another police car. From time to time, he saw Invader personnel, some in uniform but most of them not, walking the streets and talking to Earthmen just as if there was absolutely no distinction between them.

As they reached the city, the gun-carrier began passing near enough to people, and at a slow enough speed, so that Michael Wireman could be seen to be a prisoner at gunpoint. He was thunderstruck when a man leaned out of a bus window at a traffic light and deliberately spat downward, just missing his leg.

"Sit back, you," Boros growled as the gun-carrier pulled away from the light. "Think I want you torn to pieces by a mob before I can deliver you?"

"Wh—?" Michael Wireman made an astonished noise.

"It may only have been ten days, but you had plenty enough time to get as dirty as any other dissident. I wouldn't blame them for making mistakes."

Silently, Michael Wireman huddled inside the gun-carrier as they drove through the clean, bustling, suddenly cold streets of Philadelphia.

2

The interrogating officer was a great deal older than Lieutenant Boros, who had gone grimly back to his own garrison town. But he, too, might have been an older brother in that hawk-faced family, and part of that one, great unit.

That quality in the interrogating officer confronted Michael Wireman now. His feeling of helplessness was only intensified by the speed with which a dossier on Michael Wireman had appeared in the interrogating officer's hands, radiophotoed from Central Headquarters in Geneva, half a world away.

"Michael Wireman," the interrogating officer said softly, looking down at the opened folder. "Michael Wireman," he said again, as though especially intrigued. "Your father is President of the Government in Exile."

Michael Wireman nodded. The room was bare, without furnishing or decoration to catch the eye and offer it rest. There were two chairs, and a table between them. Michael Wireman had no choice but to watch the interrogating officer.

"You were parachuted into the mountains ten days ago?"

"Yes."

"From a spaceship, obviously."

"Yes."

The interrogating officer looked up. "That ship would be a vessel of the Centaurian System Organization armed forces?"

Michael Wireman fenced cautiously. "It doesn't belong to the C.S.O." He clung to the legal fiction. He understood how much trouble it might make, even now, if he did not stress that tricky point.

The interrogating officer smiled ironically. "Isn't it fascinating what can be done with international law?"

"I suppose it is," Michael Wireman said, and for some reason the interrogating officer abandoned his line of questioning in favor of another.

"Suppose we talk about you," he said. He shuffled through the papers. "You left Earth at the age of one, when your family fled to Cheiron, and have never been back. You grew up on Cheiron, among Centaurians who, descendants of Earthmen though they are, have been an independent people for generations; who have grown rich and powerful in their own right, and whose ties with Earth are tenuous in the extreme. A people with folkways as alien to you as mine would be. Were you happy?"

"Happy enough."

"Were you, really?" The interrogating officer was suddenly less than casual. "I'd have thought you'd be preoccupied with your hope of an eventual return to Earth—with your status as a member of what would have to be regarded as Earth's most important family—with your difference from the children of a prosperous and self-assertive nation which has never known defeat. A nation which would regard Terrestrial affairs as very small beer indeed, and a fervent Terrestrial patriot with a thick Centaurian accent as a rather strange kind of freak."

"You're very clever," Michael Wireman whispered.

"You're not a prepossessing boy," the interrogating officer went on. "You have funny-looking ears, and you're clumsy. You don't impress people as being particularly bright. Tell me again, Michael —were you happy?"

Michael Wireman shook his head.

"All right," the interrogating officer said gently. "When they decided to send you here, it was the answer to all your dreams, wasn't it? At last you were going back where you belonged."

There was a pause. "I was happy," Michael Wireman said, his throat aching.

"Happy," the interrogating officer said. He looked at Michael Wireman's face. "Yes, I imagine you were." He waited a little while, shuffling his papers, and said: "But now you're not. In ten days you've gone from happiness to misery. That's a sudden metamorphosis, Michael Wireman. Weren't you accepted into Hammil's group?" His glance came up. "Or wasn't Hammil exactly what you'd expected?"

Michael Wireman said nothing. He saw the Invader smile.

"You don't like Hammil, or his methods," the interrogations officer said. "You didn't like the looks of Liberty's champions, eh?"

"No." What was the good of keeping anything back?

"And they didn't like yours, I'll bet. You're lucky to be alive, you know that?"

"I know it. I'm sure he's glad I'm at least gone."

"Yes. Tell me—do you think he's already rationalized things into a belief he can become dictator of the world?"

"Yes." It hadn't, after all, been too surprising a deduction on the Invader's part.

The officer nodded slowly. "It might not be such a mad notion, at that," he murmured. "But we'll return to it. It's still you we're interested in."

Michael Wireman began to understand, again belatedly, that an Invader never asked a question without moving toward some objective beyond the obvious. He began to feel afraid of what the officer's ultimate point might be.

The interrogating officer was shaking his head. "You don't fit, Michael Wireman. You don't fit on Cheiron; you don't fit up in the mountains. I wonder . . . your father must be a very busy man . . ."

Michael Wireman bit his lip.

"You don't fit with your family . . . You don't fit anywhere, do you, Michael?"

Michael Wireman had nothing to say.

"Still . . . Would you be giving up so easily?" The interrogating officer seemed to enjoy his work. "Let's see how the pieces add themselves together. . . .

"A ship, now. A whole interstellar ship, at the Government in Exile's disposal. That seems odd. And the president's son sent back to Earth on it. Well, now. Suppose we look at the big picture."

The interrogations officer leaned forward casually. Like a man reading lecture notes, he said:

"Twenty years ago, the C.S.O. stayed out of the war. Now things are different. Now our two spheres of interest are beginning to come into conflict in all sorts of places. They've grown more powerful, and their next natural area for expansion is one we want, too. Now might be a good time for a war. So the Government in Exile—the Government in Exile, mind you, not the C.S.O.—the Government in Exile suddenly becomes rich. Rich enough to sneak a ship into the Solar System.

"Now, why would they want to do that? Well, Earth's a quiet little place, these days—well back of our frontier, well out of our boom areas. The war's over for us. We don't have this place heavily garrisoned. So, if somebody down here could be found to engage our land forces and do the dying while a C.S.O. fleet moved in to set up a blockade . . . A nice, clean, comparatively cheap blockade to keep off our relief ships until it was too late— why, then the C.S.O. would have put a very useful breach in our defenses, at practically no cost.

"And if we had somehow found out all these plans in mid-stream, why, it wouldn't have been the C.S.O. that was caught with its finger in a

very embarrassing pie. It would have been that
fanatic old Government in Exile, and the C.S.O.
might even have closed it down for us, then. Why
not? It would have officially satisfied our protest,
at the negligible sacrifice of an already shot bolt.
What do you think of that, Michael?"

Michael Wireman had nothing to say. He watched
the officer carefully.

"It could still happen, you know," the interrogations officer said. "Doesn't it upset you to think of
your family stripped of its status, Michael? Possibly interned, or at best left alone to get along on
what your father and mother could earn as private
citizens? How old is your father now, Michael? I
understand your mother's an invalid."

"Go on."

"On? Well, yes, there is more, isn't there? Because you're not worried about what might have
happened—or what you might reasonably expect
could still happen. I thought perhaps you would
be, but I see you're not. All right. Let's go on.
Let's go back to the Government in Exile's new
money, and what it does with it.

"Let's say—oh, let's say the Government in Exile finds some C.S.O. weapons for sale. Let's say
they're dropped to Hammil. Let's say a misfit boy
with a valuable last name gets run through some
C.S.O. weapons training courses, dressed in dyed
C.S.O. Navy coveralls, and dropped with the guns
so Hammil will have someone around to represent
the old government. Except that Hammil doesn't
want any strings on him. But perhaps your group
didn't know what the situation was. Did it?"

Michael Wireman was looking straight ahead.

"Boy," the interrogating officer said quietly,
"didn't anyone realize? Not even your father? If

they didn't know Hammil, couldn't they at least stop to think that the C.S.O. would have its own interests? The C.S.O. doesn't need you to be its dummy any longer. They're committed now, and they might as well go at things directly. The C.S.O. has plans for Earth after the war, and they don't include restoring a rival sovereign power here. *Nobody* wants you."

The interrogations officer added softly: "You found that out, didn't you?"

Michael Wireman nodded.

The interrogations officer shook his head. "You've really had it, haven't you?"

Michael Wireman nodded again, his eyes far away. "We went down the mountain to attack the command post this morning."

"Yes?"

"We went down the mountain. I couldn't believe it. I was positive Hammil would wipe out the rival bandit leaders first, and recruit the survivors. But we went down the mountain. I think Hammil wanted me to get killed. I didn't. We knocked over the command post, and then I found out why we'd attacked it in the first place. Hammil knew the commanding officer. He'd been in charge of Hammil's classification test."

"Oh?" The interrogations officer glanced sharply at Michael Wireman. "You know about those, do you?" But there was a definite sense that he was not surprised—that one glance had told him all he needed to know about Michael Wireman, and that now it had all only been confirmed. "You knew about the classification test system before this morning?" he asked softly.

"No. What's that got to do with it?"

The interrogations officer looked at him without

rancor or malice. "Michael Wireman, you must have realized at some point today how much you're giving us with your surrender. You're not politically illiterate. We knew the C.S.O. would move against us sometime, in some way. But now we know where and how. It's probable now—considering that it's Hammil who opposes us—that our grip on Earth will never be shaken by anyone. In another generation, terrestrials will hardly remember a time when they considered themselves an individual race. They will be members of our culture, completely; some of them will no doubt fight in the assimilation of the Centaurian System Organization, and they will be fighting to sustain our ideals, our way of life. Whatever happens now, Earth will never be the Earth you love.

"You've surrendered your childhood dreams to us, Michael Wireman. And why? Because Hammil is an egomaniacal murderer? Because if we do lose Earth, we won't lose it to your clique? You've given up your most precious aspirations for petty things like that?"

"Yes!"

"No! Don't you realize, Michael Wireman, what one thing will make a man give up his birthright?"

Michael Wireman had no answer.

"You want to fit in," the interrogations officer said. "You want to be accepted. I think we can agree that unrealized ideals would come second to that in any man. You've come to us for what your father and Hammil could never give you. And we can. You want us to classify you. You want to belong. That's why you surrendered."

Michael Wireman couldn't deny it.

The interrogations officer smiled at him kindly.

"Well, now, that's all right, Michael," he said. "We're glad to have you."

He seemed to mean it. It came to Michael Wireman that he really seemed to mean it, and this discovery in itself was so much of a spur to his emotions that, combined with everything else that had happened to him, it made his self-control desert him completely. He began to cry.

The interrogations officer left him alone for a few minutes, and that was long enough. Michael Wireman lifted his head again, feeling as though a great many things had been washed away. The interrogations officer had done an excellent, tactful job. Michael Wireman felt less guilt-ridden at this moment than he had in months.

The interrogations officer made a final entry in the dossier and closed it. He put it in the desk. "We'll arrange for you to get cleaned up, and give you a comfortable place to sleep. Then, in the morning, we'll give you the classification test, eh? By noon, you'll be one of us." The officer was plainly winding up what had become an uninteresting part of this case. He had solved Michael Wireman and now he wanted to go.

"Thank you, sir," Michael Wireman said huskily.

FOUR

1

Early in the morning, Michael Wireman stood at his window, looking down and out over Philadelphia, at the clean river, and at Camden, the twin city, across that river on the New Jersey side. The air sparkled in the sun, and the sound of a pigeon suddenly taking flight from the sill was an explosion of clear, sharp sound like the opening of a drama.

The buildings—not all of them, but most of them—were clean; scrubbed, probably, by some sort of subsonic broom of vibration that knocked grime loose from the stones. The streets were beautifully kept up. He had to look hard to find even neat patches in the surface. It was a characteristic of the Invaders to be orderly and tidy, to a degree that the C.S.O., with its cities shrouded in industrial haze, did not bother with. It was consistent with the entire Invader culture that things should be like this. A place for everything, and

117

everything in its place. A race not only of track-men but of housewives.

He wondered, with a little smile, if he would have admired the Invaders so much if their culture were not so conscious of as seemingly unimportant a thing as cleanliness. A modern civilization, equipped with total-spectrum antibiotics, automatically sterilized food and drink, and all the other matter-of-course public health byproducts of advanced medicine and food distribution, could afford to literally wallow in filth beyond the wildest extremes of savagery. There was no apparent practical reason for doing otherwise. From one point of view, it was even inefficient to divert labor-time and money away from more practical concerns.

And yet, Michael Wireman thought, would they have the Earth if they didn't? Would they have me? (Would they care about *that?*) Perhaps the measure of ultimate victory had been the length of stubble on the chins of men like Franz Hammil.

Michael Wireman stood looking out. He felt a great deal better for having had a hot bath and clean clothes to put on. But despite the night's sleep, he was still weary. The weariness would stay with him, deep in his bones, he knew, until he could become part of that crowd in the cities below, a man with a kith and a home. He had given up making comparisons with the mythical Earth of his childhood. He had only this, down there, to aspire to. It was all he wanted.

There was a knock on the door behind him. "Come in," he said, turning reluctantly as the door opened. "Yes?"

The middle-aged, spare, self-possessed man with grayed black hair carried a thick folder in his hand. He was dressed in clothes which seemed quite oddly tailored, compared to Centaurian fashions, but which were obviously expensive and conservative. He glanced at the label on the folder. "Michael Wireman?"

"Yes." Michael Wireman looked at him searchingly. This was the first Invader-classified Earthman he had ever met. He was immediately curious, and deeply intrigued.

"My name is Hobart, Mr. Wireman," the man said without offering to shake hands, and wheeled a small machine, waist-high on castered legs, into the room. The machine was housed in a beige crackle-finished case. There were dials, keys, and input jack terminals on its face, and auxiliary equipment hung from clips on its sides.

"Doctor Hobart?" Michael Wireman asked.

"That's right," Hobart said briskly, "but don't let it worry you. I'm not going to strap you down and cut out your brain."

"I didn't expect you would," Michael Wireman said.

Hobart's black eyebrows rose. "Oh. Forgive me." He smiled with a quick deprecatory skill. "Sometimes it's hard to judge how much one of you will know about the nature of the classification process."

Michael Wireman felt a flash of irritation. He was momentarily surprised by his own daring at feeling any such thing. But then he smiled thinly to himself as he thought that for this one, brief interval of time, he could be anything he pleased. It no longer mattered what his past had been— there would be a clean break away from it later today. It did not matter what he made this doctor think of him—the test would tell the doctor what to think, later today. In this respite between one life and another, one loyalty and the next, there was no code to adhere to, nothing to fear from anyone. And if he did, indeed, do something ill-advised or even inexcusable by any standard—and could he be trusted not to?—why, the test would give him absolution.

He gestured toward a chair. "Sit down, doctor," he said, sounding as mature as any man. "One of us? One of us dissidents, you mean? Are we usually presumed to be ignorant? I'm a special case, doctor. Do you get a lot of captured men to classify?"

Hobart shook his head with a quizzical glance at him. "No, no, I can't say that we do," he replied evenly. "Usually, as you know—"

"I don't know, Doctor."

"Very well, as you don't know, the dissidents want nothing so much as to be left alone. They can't cope with society or civilized mores. They hardly impinge on society at all, and so they're generally left alone." This was said a little more testily. The doctor sat down, and Michael Wireman was at him again:

"But when you do get one of them, he's full of superstitious fears about brain-washing, is that it?"

"Well, yes."

"And you came in here expecting to find another low-normal like that."

"Yes." The doctor was intrigued now. He watched closely from his chair.

"You don't like the dissidents, do you, Doctor? They make trouble. They occasionally kill someone besides one of themselves, don't they?"

"I have to admit that, yes."

"In fact, some Earthmen actively despise dissidents."

"Yes," the doctor said, and smiled a little to

himself. He had been thrown off stride, he was
plainly thinking, but now he had re-oriented himself and was ready for his first chance to regain
control of the conversation.

Michael Wireman saw the smile, and read it for
what it was. He stopped and looked thoughtfully
at Doctor Hobart. He felt fairly sure that it would
raise his stock with Hobart to tell him he'd killed
two of his fellow Earthmen in the mountains. But
the memory of his bitterness was too fresh in his
mind. And it wasn't necessary, after all, that everyone like him.

It came as a slight shock, to realize that he was
angry at Hobart. Hobart's opinion of him did not
matter, after all. Why be annoyed at him?

"Were you going to say something more, Mr.
Wireman?" Hobart asked curiously.

"No." He seemed to have run down.

"I could have sworn . . . Well, no matter . . ."
Hobart settled more comfortably in his chair. "Tell
me something about yourself, Mr. Wireman. What's
your principal hobby?" Hobart's blue eyes were
dangerously sapient.

"Hobby?"

"What do you do best, Mr. Wireman?"

"Nothing." It was an honest answer.

"Nothing at all, Mr. Wireman?"

"That's right."

Hobart's eyebrows danced. "Well, then, I think
we'd better get on with your test." He opened his
folder. There were sheaves of paper inside. "Suppose you start on some of these forms, while I get
the computer set up." He handed Michael Wireman some of the printed sheets, together with a
pencil. "Just sit down anywhere, fill in the biographical information, then go on to the test. On

this first part, just mark the direction in which you think the ultimate gear in each train will turn. It's quite simple—just mechanical comprehension."

"Simple. Yes." Michael Wireman looked down at the sheets. "It's what the computer makes of it all in relation to my other skills that counts, though."

"That's right, Mr. Wireman." Hobart turned and set the circuits of the metal box. "Don't worry, we'll have you finished in a few hours."

Michael Wireman's mouth had gone dry. Hobart was just a man with some papers and a machine. But the next few hours were important—they were vitally important—and this man, these papers, that machine, together, were what he had been seeking all his life.

"Good lord!" Hobart said. He was holding the filled-in biographical form.

Michael Wireman looked up impatiently. He was working at furious speed, completing the test forms rapidly. There were a great many of them, and he wanted to finish as soon as possible.

"You *are* related to that Wireman. I thought it was just a coincidence in names."

"It isn't," Michael Wireman admitted shortly, and went back to the forms.

"Just a minute," Hobart said with probably unintended emphasis. "That can wait a little, I think," he qualified as Michael Wireman grudged him his unwilling attention. "How did you come to get here?" Hobart pressed. "I had no idea who you were."

"You had my dossier. It's all there."

Hobart seemed completely nonplussed for the first time. He glanced involuntarily toward the manila folder, then, with a peculiar expression,

said: "I don't often bother to read them, any more."
With shutterlike speed, his normal expression was
back. "I find personal discussions more meaning-
ful, in any case." Whatever else he might do,
Hobart seemed always able to regain his chosen
position of self-containment.

"I'd rather not talk about it," Michael Wireman
said.

"Is it painful to you?"

"It's personal."

"I see. . . ." Hobart said, and perhaps he did,
for Michael Wireman was conscious, each time he
looked up during the tests from then on, of Hobart's peculiarly intent reading of the dossier.

From time to time, the computer gave Hobart
unseen sub-computations which, in some way Michael Wireman was not equipped to understand,
guided the man in administering the next battery
of tests. Hobart had a mannerism—a way of looking aside at the dials without so much as blinking—
which Michael Wireman found upset him badly.
At one point there was a rip from the latest test
form, and Michael Wireman found his pencil had
torn through it. He became unpleasantly aware of
perspiration beading his upper lip and seeping
down the walls of his chest.

From time to time, Hobart called a rest period,
and they chatted about inconsequentials Michael
Wireman began to doubt were inconsequential.

2

Hobart's carefully unblinking eyes twitched
toward the dials and back. "Mr. Wireman."

"Yes?"

"Suppose we relax for a while." Was his voice too gentle? Were his eyes too knowing?

"I'd like to go on."

"Suppose we relax."

"All right." There wasn't anything else to do, if Hobart wanted to stop.

"Good." The man registered satisfaction. "I'm curious about your life with the dissidents. It's not often we get an *objective* opinion."

The stress was definitely there. Was Hobart sneering at him?

"What about it?" Michael Wireman answered sharply.

Hobart sighed patiently. "Do you have the idea I dislike you?"

"Yes."

"Why?"

"Because I'm a dissident."

"But you're not, are you?"

"No! But you won't be easy with me until I'm classified."

"Oh?"

"You can't like me, Doctor. I don't fit, yet. I might turn out to be anything."

Hobart considered the answer seriously. "You may be right. I can't pretend I'm comfortable in your presence. I can't help thinking you were with Franz Hammil on that raid."

"Hammil," Michael Wireman said angrily, "is a slug. But he's nothing to worry about now he's lost the advantage of surprise. If Joe Newsted had the ability to make people follow him, then you'd have something up in those mountains to make your blood really run cold."

"Oh?"

"Hammil needs Newsted to get him out of trouble, because Hammil alone would kill himself in no time. Hammil doesn't quite realize that, but he's still got animal cunning enough to keep Newsted around."

"And Newsted?"

"Nobody likes Newsted. Nobody likes Hammil, either, but he hypnotizes you. You have to think that a man who puts on so many airs has to have something, underneath it all. Newsted couldn't get an idiot boy to follow him. So he has to sponge on Hammil to stay alive at all. The crippled lead the crippled, up in the mountains, but they don't do it for love of each other."

Hobart's cool eyes glanced to the dials and back.

"Is there a voice-recording input on that thing?" Michael Wireman asked sharply.

"Never mind that."

"Never *mind* it?"

"Mr. Wireman, are you here to take the test or aren't you?"

"You *don't* like me, do you?"

"No." Hobart seemed relieved. "I've decided. I think I hate you, a little bit, Mr. Wireman. You don't like the things I like. You don't think in a way I can understand. Most important, I can never say to myself: 'Anything this man can do, I can do.' "

"So we understand each other."

"No, Mr. Wireman. We've perhaps come to an agreement, but we don't understand each other. Tell me about Newsted, now. You admire Newsted to a certain extent, don't you?"

"I don't."

"You admire his unique kind of intelligence. Tell me something. What could Newsted do to overthrow Hammil?"

"Do? He could get control of Hammil's weapons. Then he could have Hammil killed. But he wouldn't last more than a day or two before someone killed him. He's not the type to lead. He doesn't have Hammil's gall. Hammil can give a suicidal order as though it were the wisdom of the ages. Newsted can't say something perfectly sensible without sounding as if he didn't trust himself."

"Let's say he could. Let's say Newsted could command followers. Then what? How would he get control of Hammil's guns, precisely?"

"He'd desert Hammil, and take a few picked men with him. He'd contact other bandits in the mountains, and recruit his own army with a promise of weapons. He'd lay out an intelligent plan of attack, surprise Hammil, and that would be that. Hammil couldn't fight his way out of a paper bag, surprised by men who know mountain tactics."

"And then, what? What would Newsted do from there?"

"He'd consolidate the mountains. He'd get more guns. He'd get some light automatic cannon, and wipe out your foothill garrisons. That would give him motorized equipment. Then, with the proper support in the air, he could do almost anything, if your troops here weren't reinforced. Particularly if he promised his men they could loot the cities."

"Is that so?"

Wireman laughed savagely. "But he couldn't do it. Even if he could lead men, the people who supply the guns and the air support won't deal with him. He's a criminal, with a record. They don't dare invest in him. They've got to have somebody they believe would fight a war, instead of raiding and retreating with the loot. They need somebody like Hammil, who wants to be Julius

Caesar. And with Newsted giving him a little help here and there, that's what he could be. If he plays his cards right. But he won't. He'll stumble, somewhere—he was born to stumble."

"That's a very interesting analysis, Mr. Wireman. Do you really think the garrison army can be overcome so easily?"

"Look, a garrison army exists to hold strong points until a reinforcing army is brought in from some reserve area. In this case, the 'Vaders here would have to hold out until troops could be brought in from their nearest base, which is bound to be months away even by ultra-drive. Now, you can be pretty sure the garrisons're calculated to be able to hold out as long as necessary. But what if the relieving force never comes? What if it's intercepted and destroyed by a hostile fleet, or, at best, delayed en route long enough for the garrisons to be pried out and a C.S.O. forward base to be established here?" His voice was rising. He became vehement. It was the one subject on which he knew he knew more than Hobart.

"You people down here have gone soft with your peacetime living. You figure the dissidents'll kill each other off, or die of disease, or get too worn down to go on. But what if the dissidents get modern weapons, and one man—just one good man, to lead them, to start the ball rolling? Who can predict, then, where it will end? The garrison army can hold them in check now, because they never attack on a broad front. But what if they do—what if thousands of men start raiding down out of the mountains at the same time—how many mobile patrols do the 'Vaders have? How many places can they protect at the same time? No, they'll have to pull in their horns, fort up, and go into a state of siege. And once *that* starts, then they're committed to waiting for the relieving force—which may never come." Michael Wireman blinked down at his fist in his open hand. His hand still tingled. And he was on his feet. It was incredible, how far he had let himself be carried away.

He took a deep breath. The doctor was staring at him peculiarly.

"This is all theoretical, of course," the doctor said softly.

"Yes, of course," Michael Wireman answered, a little dazed.

"I'm fascinated by you, Mr. Wireman, did you know? I'm fascinated by listening to what you have to say." Hobart was still apparently seated at ease, still urbane, still in complete command of himself. But there was a faint sense of renewed effort. He seemed to feel the need of exercising control over his emotions.

"The glory of combat? The thrill of shooting people down?" Wireman asked.

"Good Lord, no! No—no, it's something bigger than juvenile fantasizing, I'd hope." Now he leaned forward and did not even seem to know it. "You have no idea, do you, of what it's like to make a plan for your life and follow it? To chart a course and sail on toward the tropic island of your goal: security, position, reputation—whatever it is that you would like to take for comfort to your death-bed? How much satisfaction there is in seeing that your plan has been well founded, that you are sailing on exactly as you originally charted it, that you are the envy of others less provident than yourself?"

Michael Wireman could only look at him without understanding. If anything, he felt a certain wonder at anyone who felt so unsure of his inherent worth that he planned to circumvent his destiny, whatever it might be.

"I thought not," Hobart said with a hint of a sigh. "Take my word for it, then. People do it, and those of them who do it thoughtfully are the most successful men of their generation. They are in control of their lives, and know it. You cannot imagine how much satisfaction that can give a man—and then to hear someone like you casually juggling the foundations of the world; obliviously setting forth the exact means by which the oceans will be drained, and all our stately ships broken on the emergent shoals . . ." Hobart's voice trailed away. Now he was melancholy. Wireman could make nothing of it.

"Are you frightened, doctor?" he asked.

"Frightened?" Hobart was pale. "Frightened?" He got up suddenly, his face contorted. "Don't sneer at me, Wireman! I'm a better man than you are. I've always known where I was going. I've never made a serious mistake in getting there. I'm respected, I'm well-off, I'm well known in my field."

"That would follow—the Invaders tested you, after all." It was, Michael Wireman realized, only a smartalecky answer. He had no idea of why Hobart should be so upset, but, clearly, the man was better off than the mountain rebels. Right or wrong, Hobart was more intelligent than Michael Wireman. It followed that Hobart had good reasons for his passion. If Michael Wireman could not see them, that was his own fault. He had no right to gibe at anyone.

He was astonished to see Hobart react as if he had been stabbed.

"Damn you, *yes*, they classified me! Thirty years ago! And where would I be today, what would I have done with myself, if they hadn't? And haven't I, in thirty years, grown within myself *at all*? Am I still better fitted to be a psychometrician than anything else? I had a good singing voice, once. I am more moved by a well-performed Don Jose than I am by any of my successes, and I cannot watch a man on stage without wishing I were he! I paint—Sundays. I sculpt. I have—" It was a contemptuous grimace at himself. "—hobbies. Because it's too late, now. I'm trained. I *couldn't* start over at something else. The tests said I was a better potential psychologist than I was anything else, thirty years ago. The tests were right—I administer them now, I've handled thousands of cases and followed them up afterward, and I *know*. They were right—and I can't be reclassified now, because what would be the good of only embittering me by showing me I *ought* to study voice—at fifty. How could a society function if it had to continually reshuffle its specialists? But what can I do when I wonder if, if I have grown in thirty years, I might not have grown into some greater talent in a differently arranged world? What would I be, what would I do, if the world were changed? What might not still release me, if things were different?

"Frightened of what you've said? Of course I'm frightened! And attracted, too, Wireman—damnably attracted."

Michael Wireman stared at him. "So you're *not* happy."

"I don't know if I am or not!"

"The test . . ." He fumbled for logic. "The test

is supposed to put everyone exactly where he belongs. You even say it does. It measures you, it assesses you, it gives you what you deserve. How can you question it?"

"I'm not questioning it! I'm questioning myself—and you, and no one knows what else. I'm. . . ." Hobart was quieting again. "In the end," he said, "I suppose I'm not contented with success in only one world. I wonder if I'm unique in that respect." He turned back toward the table where the completed questionnaires were piled beside the one Michael Wireman had been working on when Hobart interrupted him.

But Michael Wireman could not let it end here, with Hobart dropping what, for Michael Wireman, was only begun.

"Wait, now," he said clumsily. "Wait. You can't just leave it at that. I'm here because I *want* to be classified. I'm here to find my place. You can't first make me doubt, and then just—"

"I wonder, now," Hobart interrupted him, speaking in a low voice as if mostly to himself and as if he had not heard. "The Invaders don't seem to have any record of such a thing in their own society. Perhaps it was a long time ago, and they've selected the strain out of their populace. And it must be a rare one even among humans." He turned back toward Michael Wireman. His glance was absorbed, thoughtful, perhaps sad.

"I'm not sure about you, Wireman. A man who can't fit into a society must logically sink down and, at best, become a parasite around its edges. But there might be times when such a man might not. There might be circumstances. There might be something in the man, or the one might depend on the other. I can't tell. My computer and

my questionnaires can't tell me. A test cannot
measure something that would invalidate its own
basis."

"What about the test, doctor?" Michael Wireman asked, possessed by anticipatory fear.

Hobart said bluntly: "You failed it, Wireman.
You haven't come anywhere near being classified
for anything. It was obvious from the start. And
you suspected it, I think. You tried to overawe me
just because I was going to give it to you. You
tried to evade the machine. You've been fighting
it every step of the way, until you'd worked yourself into a rage. You don't *want* to belong—you
think you *ought* to belong."

"Worked myself into a—!"

"Exactly, Wireman." Hobart shook his head.
"Didn't you know?" He looked narrowly at Michael Wireman. "No, I suppose not. Look here—I
don't know what you are. You may thirst for your
proper niche—but there's none for you. You've
got an above-average intelligence—not an uncom-
mon one, by a long shot—and nothing else I can
measure meaningfully. The machine says you've
got an equally low aptitude for every field of work.
You would be a run-of-the-mill worker at almost
anything you tried . . . but the world is full of
people who are only run-of-the-mill at their out-
standing aptitudes; what's the advantage to society
of having somebody around who has a talent for
universal mediocrity?" Hobart pushed on, and Michael Wireman listened in shocked silence.

"But that's not what the machine is really saying
at all—a machine only gives you an answer out of a
catalogue of possible answers that were fed into it
by its makers. If it has no exact answer in its
catalogue, it does the best it can with what it

has—just like a human being. We mustn't make
the mistake we easily could—we mustn't accept
the answer at face value just because it's an answer.

"What the machine is really saying about you is
that its makers wouldn't understand you any better than it does. You're simply not comprehensible
to anyone in the society that built this machine.
Or to a man like myself, who is not an Invader,
but a little different from an Earthman, after all
these years. I can't understand you in terms of the
Earth that will be, or the Earth that was. I don't
have to understand you in terms of the Earth that
is—I have certain standards to guide me there."

Hobart shook his head again. "You're a freak, as
far as this world goes. I've got to tell you, Wireman, that as far as my figures are concerned,
you're no more a civilizable man than Franz
Hammil."

"But I *want* to belong!" Michael Wireman cried
out.

"I'm sure you think you do. I'm sure there was
even a time when you wanted to be a good
Centaurian. But you ran away from there, just as
you ran away from Hammil. And as you'd best run
away from here."

"Are you saying that as an official of the Invader
administration?" Michael Wireman felt his gorge
rising. He now saw Hobart for a contemptible
figure—a traitor who disguised his treachery behind a mask of urbane professionalism—a traitor,
that is, more skillful than himself.

"No," Hobart said, "I'm not. I'm giving you my
professional opinion. I'm telling you that if you
stay here, you'll eventually go insane—not in social terms, as you already are, but in terms of your

individual self. You've got to run again, Michael
Wireman—you've got to keep looking."

Again? But Michael Wireman was paralyzingly
tired of it all. He did not want to go on. He
wanted only to stop. "I'm sick of running!" he
cried.

"You have no choice," Hobart prodded. "Neither I nor the Invaders can solve your problem for
you. We don't understand it. If you stay here,
we'll fumble around, trying to find something to
do with you. In the end, we'll grow annoyed because you won't cooperate with our sincere wish to
find a place for you. We'll decide you're incorrigi-
ble, and we'll dispose of you. You have to understand that superhuman forbearance, superhuman
insight, are in the province of God alone—you'll
get no help from your fellow men."

"I don't want to run!" Couldn't this supercilious
man understand that? Couldn't he see how weary
of it Michael Wireman was?

"Don't you? Are you really going to lie down in
a ditch and let what comes come?"

"I don't care—I'm tired of what people have
done to me—I'm tired of what they are! Where
am I going to go? What's left? Who's worth my
allegiance? What kind of a lousy race is this, anyway, that I was born into?" He groped for the
front of Hobart's shirt.

"It's not just one lousy race, Wireman," Hobart
said. "It's the Invaders, too. Maybe there're no
people to please you in the entire Universe. What
of that?"

"Get me out of here!" he was whispering hoarsely
with a red haze across his vision. "Get me downstairs and out of the city. I've had it now, Hobart!
I—" He realized he was being hysterical. But he

realized it only vaguely. He wanted *out*. He wanted someone to open this cage he had been born into.

Hobart was pushing back at his hands. "Guards," he whispered hoarsely. There was a pleased, almost delighted gleam in his eyes, though his face was swelling and turning red from the constriction of his collar.

"How many?"

"I don't know."

"Waiting for me?"

"No. Just guards. A squad, scattered through the building. Routine. There's been no official announcement about you."

"I'll get by them. Do you have a car? Where is it?"

"Garage downstairs."

Holding the unprotesting doctor with one hand, Wireman went through his pockets and found the keys. "Thanks."

"*Armed* guards." The doctor was vehement. It was impossible to tell whether he was threatening Wireman or warning him. Michael Wireman did not care.

"I'll get by them. Why shouldn't I?" He wondered dimly why he should, but at this moment his contempt for the entire Universe knew no bounds.

"You're not *planning*, Wireman," the doctor complained. "You'll get caught. Watch out. You're only reacting. That's no good."

"It feels good, Hobart. It feels fine."

He twisted more of the doctor's shirt. "I'm going to have to put you under for a while." He reached for the doctor's neck. "Carotid pressure. You'll be all right after a while. This is one of the pretty things I was taught to use on my enemies."

Hobart's eyes were bright and staring. "Smash the computer," he whispered as he felt the flow of oxygen into his brain diminishing. "Got tape in it—your plans—luck . . . fascinating . . ."

Michael Wireman let him slump back over a settee. In all his time on Earth, he had yet to use one bit of his training against an Invader. He no longer cared.

He was perfectly aware that he was not thinking. Anything that spared him making decisions was welcome to him now. He kicked out at the Invader computer and smashed it joyfully, eviscerating it of its tape and touching a match to the tumbled coils, watching the record of what he was writhe like a snake in a furnace. Then, without a backward glance, a pause or a plan, he ran out through the door so filled with tension that he barely restrained himself from howling like a wolf.

Standing some distance down the otherwise empty corridor, half-turned away from the door, an Invader trooper obliviously stood between Michael Wireman and the world.

FIVE

1

The guard was a young man, his uniform impeccably pressed, his belt and boots as slick as the wax he had carefully worked into the leather. He was a garrison soldier—it was possible he had never fired a shot in anger. His bearing and the condition of his equipment were the end result of a tradition that had been handed down through the military generations: in the special cave where the spears and shields were kept under the shaman's magical protection; around the fires in front of the skin tents; in the barracks; in the dormitories of the transport spaceships that had brought his race to Earth. From the first day that the first individual of his race had followed the profession of arms, the lore had been accumulating: the care of an arrow's shaft; the daubing of grease on the bowstring. The lampblack on the gunsight at the practice range. The spit and the flannel cloth on his boots before inspections. The white clay on the webbing of his parade uniform belt. All the little tricks, the accumulation of an arcana which, when the books are closed on the Universe, may prove to be the only body of folklore spontaneously common to an intelligent, combative life, white, green, or armored in the rudimentary scales of what were once lizards on a world that aged and died before the Earth was born.

Michael Wireman peered at him through eyes that were hazed with turmoil. His body was swimming with glandular secretions that made his senses over-react sharply, filling his ears with sounds normally unnoticed, and dazzling his eyes with light they ordinarily filtered down. He could hear the sound of his own blood pumping rapidly through the blood vessels around his ears. He did not blink. If he had been in a jungle, no enemy could have approached him stealthily, no shadow could have stirred unnoticed anywhere in range of his vision. His nostrils flared stiffly, and his mouth was open to supply his lungs with every possible cubic inch of the oxygen his racing blood demanded. His body was putting up an effort which would exhaust him for hours afterward, but if Michael Wireman had been in the primeval jungle, he could then have clambered into a tree, wedged himself safely out of reach of his rival predators, and slept the necessary time away.

Now he took soundless steps forward. The polished composition tile of the floor did not rustle with the sound of dead leaves underfoot, or break with the crackle of dry sticks.

The young guard hardly realized how many men had stretched their ingenuity to assure that he would be the best-looking soldier in the best company in the best regiment of the best division of the best army in the Universe. He felt the stiffening of the tradition all up and down his ramrod backbone, but if he had been asked, he would have said that fighting, and not passing inspections, was a soldier's occupation. It would have been a little bit beyond him as yet to understand that passing inspections—assuming the shape of the ideal, acquiring the symbolic stature—was exactly a soldier's business. A soldier had, in a very real sense, failed when his mere appearance no longer maintained discipline among the people he was sent to keep in order. A soldier who fired his weapons at anything but training targets was already a living admission of defeat.

Michael Wireman came up behind him, turned him with one hand on his shoulder, and killed him outright with a blow of his other hand. He did it with the stiffened, extended fingers of his right hand, braced by the thumb into a deadly wedge, driven against the young guard's trachea. An assassin's trick, older than soldiering.

The young guard collapsed, falling toward Michael Wireman with a contorted face and a choked, gurgling cough as his knees buckled. He fell into Michael Wireman's arms, and for a brief moment Michael Wireman could feel his heart still trying to beat. Then it, too, choked, as the oxygen-starved brain gave up communication with it.

Michael Wireman stared from side to side over the dead trooper's shoulder. Then he automatically and awkwardly dragged the body backward into a closet. He shook his head violently, though it was the fingers of his right hand that tingled.

He stripped the body awkwardly, half-exasperated at its loose-jointed clumsiness, half-terrified at having killed a man with his hands. Before now, he

had had the saving agency of a mechanism between the action of his hand on a trigger and the
resulting deaths of men who might have been
saved by a cartridge's mis-firing, by a bullet's being
out of true—by any one of a dozen things that
might conceivably have happened. He had thought
he understood what it was to have killed a man.
He found that he had been wrong.

The uniform was still warm with the dead man's
heat as Michael Wireman put it on. The belt had a
worn crease to show where Michael Wireman had
tightened it a notch farther than usual. Abruptly,
the remaining energy drained out of him like dirty
water.

He stood stock-still in the closet, his feet awkwardly placed to straddle the dead man's. His
hands were clenched and his face was covered
with perspiration. He was surprised to learn how
badly he was affected. In training, he had learned
that throat-crunching trick and many others, carefully absorbing each deadly lesson in applied phys-
iology with an enthusiasm born of a life-time's
innocuity. The thing was, somewhere in the back
of his mind he hadn't really expected it all to
work.

He pulled the unfamiliar sidearm out of its polished holster and looked at it curiously. He was
not acquainted with weapons as a general class.
He had been trained only in the standard Centaurian
System Organization arms, and even the C.S.O.,
by devious and attenuated trails to be sure, could
trace its cultural lineage back to Earth. This Invader pistol was something else again.

It seemed to be a projectile weapon—whether
powered by explosives or compressed propellants
was not immediately apparent—and there seemed

to be a slide around the chamber of the short, heavy-caliber barrel. There was a simple ratchet safety. This he moved to the off position, and then tried to work the slide. Pushing it forward did nothing. Pulling it back produced a slight movement. He pulled harder, and the slide came back, urging itself upward at the same time. It turned out to be hinged under a hemicylindrical sleeve, folding as it carried back, and as it reached maximum fold, a cartridge flew out of the chamber and clattered on the closet floor. Another cartridge popped up out of the clip and lay in the receiver. Michael Wireman eased the slide down, fighting spring tension that tried to snap the slide forward. Naturally enough, his excessive caution made the cartridge wedge in the receiver. The pistol jammed, its slide refusing to throw home. From a compact piece of precision machinery, the pistol turned into an awkward construction of frozen metal.

A drop of perspiration splashed into the open receiver. Michael Wireman wiped at it clumsily with the tip of a forefinger. He tugged at the slide, but somewhere in the internal machinery a follower cog had locked. The designer perhaps ought to have allowed for amateurish hands. Perhaps he had deliberately tried to design a weapon only a trained man could use.

Michael Wireman set his teeth, inserted his left index fingertip in the receiver, and pried the cartridge around. The slide smashed down. He worked it again—quickly, this time—ejected the probably deformed cartridge, and re-holstered the sidearm. He put his broken finger in his mouth for a moment, tasting blood. There were smears of it all over the gun, and several drops on the floor. He had been careful enough not to get any on his uniform, but he had to bandage up his finger somehow.

He searched the broom closet for a clean rag, and finally found one that would do. Tearing a strip off, he wound it around the fingertip, split the end with his teeth, and tried to tie it neatly. It came out a botch, already beginning to soak through, but there was no hope of doing better. And he did not have all the time in the world. The doctor might give an alarm at any moment. A change of guards might be due—anything might happen.

He looked down at the dead Invader between his feet. The joy of action was fading out of Michael Wireman's mind. He was losing momentum. The delight of finally accomplishing something had propelled him this far. But now it was gone.

He put one hand on the broom closet door handle, and stopped. But he couldn't stay in here forever.

He opened the door and stepped out. The hallway was empty. Holding his crippled hand away from his body with the fingers curled into a throbbing fist to hide the sopping bandage, he began to walk toward the elevator on legs that seemed jointless and ten yards long.

2

The elevator was crowded. A dozen blank faces stared directly at him through the opening doors. Michael Wireman almost turned and ran.

"Down," the operator said impatiently. He was a civilian employee—an Earthman in an adaptation of the Invader army uniform—but he spoke in the Invader language.

"Y-yeah," Michael Wireman croaked. He pushed forward, turning awkwardly, and the operator slammed the door shut. The knot of people in the elevator—none of them were Invader army personnel —readjusted themselves to give him a minimum amount of room. His left hand was jammed against his side, and the broken bone grated inside the skin of the first joint. He could not shout. He was nearly sick, instead.

"Garage, please," he said huskily, remembering just in time that he wouldn't be getting off at the main floor with everybody else.

"This ain't the garage elevator," the operator said peevishly. "Get off at the main floor and take the car at the end of the lobby. You new here, or somethin'?"

An aging woman with purple-tinted white hair, the shoulder pad of her tailored business suit crushed against Michael Wireman's bicep, had apparently been looking casually up at his face. "What's the matter, soldier?" she said crisply. "You don't look well." She was studying him narrowly now. "Pale."

It was not a matter of simple pallor. The damning fact was that Michael Wireman simply was neither thin enough, nor angular enough. Most important, his skin pigmentation was two shades too light. None of this mattered so long as no one looked at him too long. But in another moment the woman would re-interpret her impression of pallor. She would begin to consider the prominence of his ears, and the roundness of his nose.

"It's none of your damn business how I feel, Earthie," Michael Wireman growled. "Mind your manners."

There was a perceptible stiffening in all the

passengers. The woman's jaw dropped for an instant, then snapped shut as she stared grimly toward the front of the elevator. What Michael
Wireman had done was an incredible breach of
courtesy. There was something shocking in this
sudden reminder that the Invaders were not, after
all, simply a group of firm but benevolent friends
who had taken over the management of Earth's
affairs for the benefit of both parties concerned. It
was totally unfair.

The elevator stopped at the main floor in chilly
silence. Someone's foot came down heavily on Michael Wireman's boot as the crowd spontaneously
surged forward and around him. The operator
dropped the car two inches, apparently by accident, just as Wireman was stepping out. He nearly
fell, and the operator sniggered into a handker-
chief and then blew his nose loudly.

Michael Wireman glared at him. He was ready
to growl, when he suddenly remembered that he
was not in fact an Invader. He turned toward the
garage elevator.

He stopped halfway there, and looked toward
the street entrance. The civilian employees were
lining up at the inevitable pass-out desk, filing
past a time clock, flashing badges. An occasional
Invader passed through a similar setup, showing
identification. Michael Wireman had the dead
guard's ID cards, of course, with the dead guard's
full face and profile photographs on them.

He turned and finished walking to the end of
the lobby. His hand was bursting.

The garage elevator was automatic, and empty.
Its controls were marked only in the Invader al-
phabet. That ought to mean something, Michael

Wireman thought, but he could not reason it out.
He punched the proper button before he understood that the general run of civilians were not
permitted in the garage.

That might not be so bad. The doctor's keys in
his pocket thus became a sure sign that the doctor
was above the general run, and that might be
useful.

But it also had to mean that there would be
military personnel stationed in the garage, to control access.

Oh, God! Michael Wireman cried to himself,
it's so bloody *complicated!*

The elevator stopped, and the door folded back
into itself. He was facing a desk with a bored
Invader corporal sitting behind it, a grizzled, tired-
looking man, with heavy creases in his face, a nose
that had broken out in florae a long time ago, and
a thick roll of jowl under his chin. He looked at
Michael Wireman. "Well?"

The elevator opened on a concrete balcony with
a pipe railing. The corporal's back was to this
railing, and behind him was the main garage floor,
with about fifty vehicles parked among the struc-
tural pillars. A flight of cement steps began at the
right of the elevator and led down to the floor.
About half the vehicles were civilian automobiles.
The remainder, in their own section, were military riot cars, light trucks, and the like. There was
a background of motor noises and metallic bang-
ing. Mechanics in drab coveralls were scattered
throughout the garage, working on various cars.

Michael Wireman stepped out of the elevator,
his hand digging in his pocket. "Pickin' up Doctor
Hobart's car," he said. "He wants it out front."
Would an Invader private soldier run errands for

an above-the-general-run Earthman? Michael Wireman brought out the keys and held them so the
Invader could see them.

He held them in his left hand, streaked with
blood, the futile rag of bandage twisted around the
smashed fingertip, with blood on his uniform trousers around the pocket.

He had simply forgotten. This was the one part
of his escape that he had rehearsed ahead of time
in his mind. He had not known what the physical
circumstances in the garage would be, but he had
known all along that the keys and Hobart's name
would be his only real credentials. He had kept
this firmly in mind, decided on every intonation of
every word, and pre-set the expression of his face.
The sight of the Invader staring directly at him
had triggered the sequence.

The Invader was staring thunderstruck at the
bloody hand. "What the devil happened to *you?*"
he asked.

"I smashed it in the slide of a gun," Michael
Wireman said dully, watching his hand sinking
down automatically to his side. He seemed to have
abandoned conscious control of every part of his
body. He nearly staggered. But his mind was racing.

It wasn't taking the Invader long to recover. It
was simply that Michael Wireman had presented
him with a situation neither his training nor his
experience had ever led him to expect. He was
already reaching for the buttons set into the top of
his desk, and his other hand was edging toward his
holster.

"This gun," Michael Wireman said, casually holding it flat in his hand, not actually fitting the butt
to his palm, or his finger to the trigger. "See the
way it's all smeared up?" He kept the muzzle

straight on the corporal's paunch, which was exposed by the man's half-rising crouch.

The Invader could not get his eyes off the end of the pistol. His hands stopped moving. And Michael Wireman still did not make the mistake of giving him a clear-cut situation to react to. If Wireman had come out with a flat statement that he was an escaping prisoner, the corporal at this point would have given the alarm without stopping to think, and charged him even if the gun had been firmly held in Wireman's hand.

"Pretty dumb of me, hunh?" He held the gun out toward the man, and no one at any distance would have seen anything but one man offering something to another.

The corporal slowly began what was now for him the complicated process of sitting back down in his chair.

"I got it workin' again, though," Michael Wireman went on. "Gee, Corp," he said with apparent inanity, "ain't you gettin' pretty close to retirement age? Must be gettin' just about ready to hang it up, ain't you? Man, that's the life—sit home and drink beer all day—nothin' to do but collect the ol' pension check every so often."

He had the Invader hypnotized, now. The corporal was staring at him in fascination, not knowing what to make of him but possessed by a conviction of menace. Which might turn out to be entirely a figment of the corporal's imagination. The corporal did not want to appear a fool. Nor did he want to die, if he was not a fool. Wireman's last few sentences were sinking in.

"Say," Wireman said, "I ain't never been down here before. Which one of those cars belongs to Hobart? I don't want to keep him waitin', you know; wouldn't look good on my record." He did not reholster the pistol.

The Invader corporal could not now rid the forefront of his brain of the pistol in Michael Wireman's hand. It was obvious he was trying, but the Invader corporal was old enough and experienced enough to know what heavy-caliber slugs could do to a man at short range. He was brave enough, but not masochistic. If he had had with him now the young guard whom Michael Wireman had killed upstairs, he would have waited until the youngster had jumped first, and he would then have been able to do something himself. But he was alone, and he was getting very near retirement.

"It's that one, back there," he said, making an ambiguous gesture toward the parked civilian cars.

"*Which* one, Corp?" Michael Wireman asked, peering so closely past the corporal's head that his eyes had to move only a fraction to the right before they moved back again.

The corporal, who had been hoping, now had exhausted hope. "Follow me," he said, getting up carefully. "I'll show you."

"Gee, Corp," Michael Wireman said, "that's swell of you. I mean, takin' up your time with me. I figure you're a pretty busy man. Like, for instance, you wouldn't wanna waste any of it stoppin' to talk to any of those grease-monkeys whilst we're crossin' the floor, hunh?"

The corporal shook his head briefly.

Michael Wireman smiled. He studied the holster of the corporal's sidearm. Like the dead guard's, it was a dress rather than an action holster, with a flap and a catch. Only a man with the advantage of surprise could draw from it quickly enough to point his pistol at a nearby enemy. Very few In-

vader personnel on Earth were in sufficient practice
as combat soldiers to even contemplate such a move.

Think of an army of two million men, and you
think of two million lean-faced, cold-eyed killing
veterans, weapons held ready. It came to Michael
Wireman that all this time, even while the learned
phrases about garrison duty and occupation troops
had slipped so glibly from his tongue, the back of
his mind had been haunted by the image of just so
many hardened, unforgiving men. But out of even
a combat army of two million, only two hundred
thousand at a time are in the lines, and only half
will ever see any sort of combat. Nine soldiers out
of ten feed, clothe, arm, transport, doctor, pay
and support the tenth. These, too, are combat-
hardened veterans—first-class specialists—but not
at killing.

And in an empire such as the Invaders', where
trouble ever brews on some frontier, the great
bulk of the first-class specialists were long-ago gone
to where they were needed. On peaceful, consoli-
dated Earth, the veterans were senior officers and
sergeants—some of them. Even the basic riflemen
were fresh out of conscript training. The second
lieutenants were college boys. There were military
police emergency squads, but they were billeted
apart in strategically located barracks. And what
old-line administrative personnel there were, were
not first-class—nor even second, most of them.

No Invader on earth, except the handful who
had brought Michael Wireman into this building
yesterday, could yet be expected to know that a
trained, determined, inexperienced—unpredictably
dangerous—and ingenious hostile fighting man had
been dropped on the surface of the world. If someone had asked the corporal here if he knew there

was such a thing as the Free Terrestrial Government in Exile, he would unhesitatingly have answered No. If someone had told him it was housed on Cheiron, in the Centaurus System, he would have directed his perfunctory curse at the C.S.O., which he expected would be his nation's next enemy.

The corporal had been on garrison duty too long. It was not his function to fight. Earth was a good billet in a succession of good billets, its people successfully reclassified and in their second generation under Invader administration. Many of them had no experience of any other working social system. That war was over; finished; done—of all the people in this world, only Michael Wireman could have believed otherwise.

No one could blame the corporal for silently walking across the garage floor with Michael Wireman sauntering behind him. Michael Wireman's pistol lay lightly in its holster, the unfastened flap held down by the unobtrusive pressure of his ready arm. The corporal's own holster flap was firmly closed. It might as well have been said that the corporal was unarmed. No one could blame him for leading Michael Wireman to the proper car, instead of trying to confuse him by pretending to make a mistake. The corporal never thought of that. He was not on a war footing, and he was statistically correct—the odds against war coming to him had been two and a half billion to one.

3

Michael Wireman felt a tuned wire vibrating somewhere in his mind. It was singing with strain, and he visualized it as being fiery red, with blurred outlines that smoked.

They would execute him if they caught him, he understood. Or they might smash him down instead of bothering to attempt recapture and the foregone conclusion of a trial. They would do it not because he was their enemy, but because he was a murderer.

He felt like a murderer. It had seemed so straightforward, before the fact. Here is the enemy, standing between you and safety. Get him out of the way. And because he is as young and strong as you are, give him no advantage. But now the thing was done, and it would take a long time for Michael Wireman to assimilate it.

He liked the Invaders. Certainly, he liked the ones he'd encountered personally far better than he liked Franz Hammil. If he had not been taught as a child to think of the Invaders as subhuman brutes and butchering vandals, he might have liked them less now. If all Earth had not been dinned, before the war, with similar propaganda, all Earth might not have taken as well to the occupation as it was now doing. The simple, natural fact was that individual Invaders were intelligent, friendly people by nature; the contrast to the blood-flecked monster on the wartime propaganda poster was too much for reason to bear. If all Earth, and Michael Wireman, had been taught instead that even friendly people can destroy freedom, and that freedom is worth more than security, it might have been a different matter.

What kept Michael Wireman in motion now, instead of leaving him paralyzed with indecision, was as simple an urge to flight from danger as had driven every other evildoer before him. At this moment he had no ideals, and no political sophistication. He was running, and doubling back, and racking his brain for one ingenious trick after another—not for his convictions, but for his life.

The corporal stopped at the doctor's car. "Here," he said.

Michael Wireman nodded. "Okay. Slide the door open." They were in among the cars, now. There was even less likelihood of anyone's noticing anything wrong.

The corporal obeyed him. He backed away at a gesture from the pistol Michael Wireman had taken out again, and stood at a safe distance while he watched this bloody vandal peer into the car and try to fathom the controls.

They seemed simple enough. The car, unlike the pistol, after all was of human manufacture to human specifications. Michael Wireman nodded again. "Good enough," he said. "Turn around."

The corporal knew what was coming. He turned, but he began to run. Michael Wireman had to take four quick, pantherish strides after him before he could stun him with the gun butt.

The sound of their feet had been loud in the narrow space between the cars. Michael Wireman crouched, gun held ready. Then he laughed noisily. "Watch your step, there!" he guffawed. "Don't go tripping over your big feet again."

If any of the mechanics within earshot had heard the scuffle, they went back to what they were doing. Michael Wireman eased his way into the doctor's car, and slipped the key into the ignition lock. As he looked out through the windshield, he saw a bored private standing in front of the corporal's vacant desk at the elevator doors. Someone who probably needed permission to pass into the garage, and was waiting for the corporal to come back from the toilet and check him through.

Michael Wireman thumbed the starter.

As he was rolling toward the ramp that led up to street level, the alarm finally went off. A cacophony of bells filled the garage and presumably the rest of the building. Hobart had probably decided to turn in an alarm at last—there was no way of being sure exactly who had done it. Nor did it matter, now. Slow, slow, the entire system, at its garrison pace. As the car rumbled by a pillar, it passed a poorly maintained bell that was not even ringing.

But enough of them were so that Michael Wireman's foot stabbed blindly down on the accelerator, and he pulled the wheel too hard as he turned onto the ramp. The power steering betrayed him, and the car careered along the ramp wall, tires squealing and metal shearing, with Michael Wireman rebounding from the wheel to crack his head hard against the doorpost, jouncing forward again into the wheel, clutching for it desperately, his head lacerated, his ribs battered, finally regaining control as the car, its entire left side beaten in and the front fender cutting inexorably into the tire, charged up toward the street.

Shocked and dizzy, blood running into one eye, Michael Wireman fought the car out past an open gateway where another checkpoint had been located in the first few years of the occupation. Shouts came up the ramp behind him, but no shooting. The mechanics had no firearms, of course. The soldier patiently waiting at the elevator, unless he had been on guard duty, had not been armed either.

The car floundered down the street, dragging a chrome strip that had been peeled back like a shaving. Michael Wireman could not get it to accelerate, though he trod on the pedal as hard as he could and made sure the transmission was properly set. He did not know about what was happening to the left front wheel, but as he swung into the nearest cross street, snarling traffic, the tire freed itself for a moment and he shot ahead precipitously, snapping his head back. As he straightened the car the tire caught again and the car shuddered down to thirty miles per hour, throwing him forward. The steering wheel was yielding plastic, but it had to maintain a minimum firmness if it was to be of any use. It broke his nose.

At this point, he heard the first shot fired in his direction—by the intersection traffic policeman, obeying a policeman's instincts. The shot was into the air, a warning, but Michael Wireman could not know that. His face a mask of agony, his vision a field of clotting red, he threw the car into a narrow alley—not even the Invaders had yet been able to re-make Philadelphia completely—and, as he passed between the blank-faced building walls, he flung up the door on the passenger's side. Driving with his nearly helpless left hand, his left foot on the accelerator, he slid over and desperately searched for a crack between the buildings—for anything into which he could flee.

He saw it—a gap between an old building and the green-painted board fence around the excavation for a new one—and jumped out of the car, leaving it to dash itself along another wall's flank until it struck something and, he hoped, decoyed pursuit for one, perhaps for two or three, minutes.

He rolled over and over on the alley's narrow

sidewalk, tumbling expertly to cushion his fall, until he broke a rib against the stanchion of a No Parking sign. Sobbing for breath, he dragged himself erect and stumbled into the welcome gap.

The footing was broken, cracked by the demolition of the building that had stood where the excavation now was. Keeping his balance by continually striking his right hand against the boards, he floundered down the narrow passageway, hoping now for still another corner to turn. He had never expected to get out of the city in the car. He had never expected to keep it for more than a few blocks—its usefulness had ended the instant he was out of the headquarters building—but he had thought that he would be free to plan his flight and his ultimate destination—to choose a cranny and take time to make his next move, whatever that might prove to be.

Now he needed shelter hurriedly—shelter not for the moment, but for days. Now he was again nearly ready to give up.

Shelter offered itself to him. He emerged into a dim, tiny alcove overrun with rubbish. A short flight of steps led up to a partially opened door. On the door, lettered in faded paint from the lost day when there had been access for truck deliveries to this courtyard, was:

"*Mrs. Lemmon's Teashop. Home Baking and Pastries.*"

Standing on the grimed wooden steps, putting down a saucer of milk for a starveling cat, was an elderly woman with incredulous eyes. She stared at this apparition from some universe not her own, and could not think of how to react.

"Good Heavens!" she exclaimed. "What is it? What's happening?"

Michael Wireman could see no choice. If he tried to tell her he was an Invader trooper, she would find out the truth in minutes.

"I'm a Free Earthman!" he panted. "Escaped from 'Vader headquarters!"

"*Free* Earthman! A *rebel?*" Indignation filled her plump-cheeked face. "*Go away! Get out* of here!"

But someone was already plunging down the passageway behind him. Michael Wireman could hear the clatter of approaching bootsoles. In another moment, the runner would round the corner of the alcove.

Michael Wireman fumbled for his sidearm, but as he spun back around, dizziness tripped his feet so that he fell backwards, catching himself by one shoulder against the railing of the steps, his bloody head flung back, his watering eyes staring hopelessly straight up into the woman's.

"Why, you're hurt!" the woman cried, "What's been done to you?"

Michael Wireman's cheeks were masked in blood, except where the tear-tracks of pain had washed them. " 'Vaders—'Vaders . . ." he panted. "Interrogated me—tortured . . . beat me . . . broke loose. . . ."

"Why, you poor boy!" the woman exclaimed. "Those brutes! Here—hurry—get inside. Hide in the cellar." She pulled him up as best she could, and pushed him toward the door. Michael Wireman staggered gratefully inside.

4

Mrs. Lemmon set her purse-mouthed lips. Then she carefully bent over the saucer of milk, not permitting herself to feel the excited patter of her heart. Coaxing the frightened cat, she began calling "Here, kitty—*here*, kitty—here. . . ." She sighed heavily with relief—as she imagined she ought to—when the animal padded out from behind the box where it had taken shelter. Her first fright was already being replaced by a roseate intoxication. This was exactly like the sort of thing that happened to her heroines in the entertainment romances.

It was perfectly true, and she was completely aware of it, that her heroines gave shelter to handsome young Invader officers pursued by Centaurian agents, rather than the reverse. But the romances had starved her so for even the faintest real approximation of the basic story device that now, in her need, in her realization that this opportunity lost could never come again, she was entirely capable of making the inversion. To have betrayed the boy would have given her a moment of glory, it was true. But to protect him was to protract the delicious moment—to actually be a *conspirator* for days—perhaps for weeks. The thought of what retribution might come weeks from now was not something that could affect her decisions at the present moment.

Mrs. Lemmon remained bent over, talking to the lapping cat, as an Invader trooper, rifle at the ready, burst into the alcove.

The man was a member of the M.P. emergency riot force, despatched now from one of the various strategic points in the city, and fanning out in accordance with an established plan. It was true that he had not seen active duty in years, but the riot squads were made up of tough veterans who maintained a high unit morale and fraternized very little with the natives. This man was typically hard-looking, typically decisive; he knew his job was to flush the quarry at any reasonable risk to himself. His first jump carried him to the center of the alcove, crouched, rifle up, ready to fire at the first human thing that moved.

The cat squalled and ran away again. The woman straightened indignantly, nearly drawing fire. Only the trooper's razor-keen training saved her. Michael Wireman, in an analogous situation, would probably not have been able to keep himself from thumbing the trigger.

The trooper threw one searching look around the alcove. If he had had any reason to believe his quarry had chosen this route in preference to any of the others available, or if this had been the first or second year of the occupation, he might have investigated further. But he did not. "I nearly killed you, you know it?" he growled at the harmless native woman, to relieve his tension, and ran on.

Mrs. Lemmon watched him go, her watery eyes narrowed. It seemed to her now that she had always known—oh, yes, she had too! she affirmed to herself—that these Invaders were too good to be true.

SIX

1

There was a cubicle washroom—a grimy, rust-stained, acrid place—at the foot of the steps down into the tea room's littered cellar. Michael Wireman braced his abdomen against the edge of the washbowl and, sucking air between his flattened lips, half mopped, half pulled the sticky crust from his cheeks and forehead. As the congealed blood was scrubbed away it exposed a forehead gash that obviously needed stitching. There were enormous staring bruises around his eyes, where the blood from his shocked capillaries had leaked under the skin and coagulated. The crushed bones of his nose seemed to be stabbing their splintered ends directly into his forebrain.

He stared at himself in the specked mirror, appalled at the sight of fresh blood flowing in an oily sheet down from the long split in his scalp where his skull peeped pink-white between the curled-back edges. My God, he thought, what

have I done to myself? What has brought me to
this?

He was in severe pain. He very nearly enjoyed
it. At this moment, in a certain degree of safety,
he honestly did not care whether he was caught or
not. It seemed to him that if there were justice in
the world, he ought not to be here now. The
woman ought not to have given him shelter, the
garage corporal ought to have been able to capture
him, and, most important, the young Invader guard
ought not to have died.

What unimaginable rules could motivate a Universe in which a man of good will and high purpose could become a killer with a face like Death
itself? On what scale had it been decided that
Michael Wireman's escape was worth another man's
life?

It seemed only proper to Michael Wireman that
nearly unbearable pain should punish him. He
had come ravening out into the corridors like a
predator charging from bay, and this now seemed
to him so petty, so purely selfish an act that he
was unable to reconcile it with a rational world.

On what grounds could he have been justified
in felling another intelligent being, and crushing
his life out with an unwarned blow and a crunch of
cartilage that would haunt him forever? The sound
was in his ears now—he could hear it as though
the dead man died again beside him. No living
thing deserved to be brought so low as to make
that ugly sound. He had robbed that man of all
living dignity and destiny. And for what? So Michael Wireman could run free for another little
while? Who was Michael Wireman, to deserve
that sort of price? And that sort of damnation.

He began pawing half-heartedly through the

sketchy first-aid supplies in the washroom cabinet. He knew that in a short while the Invaders would discontinue their attempts to make an immediate capture, would conclude that he had found shelter, and would fall back on an inescapable slow search that could not help but root him out sooner or later—soon, if he stayed this near the headquarters that would be the focal point for the expanding boxes of a square search.

And so, what? he cried out in his mind. What is this world, and who am I, and what set of rules can possibly include us both? Where did I first go wrong, to begin this chain of terrible errors?

A less passionate, more stable man than Michael Wireman would have worked it out eventually. A less analytical man would not have bothered. Almost any kind of man but Michael Wireman might have either arrived at some solution or felt no need for it. But all these other men would not have lived in such a way as to be where Michael Wireman was now.

Down in that washroom, Michael Wireman nearly surrendered for the last time. He might have, and the world would never have heard of it. Thousands of men like him must have come to moments like his, in the world's history, and dissolved into lifelong passivity. But of those thousands, some few had not.

Moving in reflex and for almost no other reason, he began doctoring himself. He packed cotton into his nostrils, and wrapped three tight adhesive bandages around his crushed finger. He did what he could about his forehead, which was to paint the edges of the cut with iodine and then quickly press a row of adhesives across it. Here he was not so successful, for the adhesive kept pulling loose, but by repeatedly wiping the skin dry and applying bandages as quickly as possible, he eventually managed to get something that held together. It still looked slapdash, but at least he could now clean his face. That left only his ribs to be attended to, and he was peeling off his stained uniform blouse when he heard a hesitant knocking at the washroom door.

"Yes?" His nasal voice surprised him.

"Is that you, in there?" the woman asked through the door. "Are you all right?"

"Yes." What was he going to do with her? How long could she be depended on?

"Do you need any help from me?"

Help? He hadn't thought in those terms. In his mind, he was still completely alone. "Why, yes—do you have a roll of adhesive tape anywhere?"

"There's a box of bandages in the medicine cabinet," she suggested tentatively.

"I'm afraid those won't do." He opened the washroom door, and she stepped back hastily. "I have a broken rib, I think."

"Oh. Oh, my!"

He was instantly suspicious of her stagey reactions. He was unable to decide whether she was trying to lead him on for a time and then turn him in for a reward, or what.

She brightened. "I'll go to the drugstore and buy some! It isn't far."

"No!" That came out of him automatically and violently. "They'll have—" He stopped short. "Do you have any plumber's tape?"

"Oh, yes! You can see this is a very old building. They're going to tear it down soon. The pipes are forever leaking. I'll go and get it."

"Thank you." The last thing he wanted to do in

the world, right now, was to remind her she was on the wrong side of the law. The 'Vaders would as a matter of course be checking drugstores for purchases of first aid supplies; they were certain to have found traces of his blood in the wrecked car.

She walked quickly away before he could decide whether he even trusted her out of his sight or not. And he was instantly aware of how much his indecision had cost him.

As soon as she was gone, he was alone again. And, alone in a reeking little room in which he might conceivably be shot down into a huddle on the floor, he realized that his life depended on a woman who was totally untrustworthy and who was out of his control.

He was not frightened by the thought. He was indignant at it; at the thought of the world's being so constructed that life itself was at the mercy of whim and hysteria—that lies could save life and truths destroy it; that to expect mercy for goodness in this world was to embrace a suicidal folly.

Nothing happened to Michael Wireman by the time the woman returned; nothing a camera or a reporter could have seen and recorded as a lesson for the world. He had merely been alone for a little while.

He had closed the door again. She knocked on it timidly. "I—I found it. Are you still there?"

"Yes, I am," he said evenly. He opened the door and took the tape. "I wonder if you could help me?" He had his arms raised, and she began diffidently wrapping the tape tightly around his livid chest as he turned slowly.

Because it was important for him to know this

person as well as he could, he studied her face carefully. He saw the too-symmetrical spot of rouge on each cheek, the lipstick on the creased mouth, the powder over the dry and sagging skin. Her hair had been rinsed with a bluish tint, and this surprised him. But inasmuch as everything else about her seemed carefully conventional, he decided that this was probably normal with terrestrial women.

There honestly did not seem to be anything out of the ordinary about her, and he found himself embarrassed that this was so. It seemed to him that she would have a right to resent his passing that sort of judgement on her. It seemed to him that there was something essentially regrettable in her being that way, and in his ability to see it. Of course, perhaps he was wrong.

But what of it, one way or the other? If he was right, had he made her what she was? And if he was wrong, was it worse to act in accordance with his judgement than to decide he might be wrong and not act at all? He had been making mistakes all his life, and now if he was going to live much longer he had to do *something*. Could it hurt to make a few more mistakes? And—and—for the first time in his life, this thought came to him— perhaps he *was* right. If he were, it would be a real disservice to her for him to act as if he were not. They were dependent on each other now— but not equally, for he was better equipped to flee from Invader justice than she. He was responsible for her.

He had been turning slowly around and around all this time, pulling gently against the woman's grip on the unrolling doughnut of tape, and studying her during those intervals when he was facing her. At no time had he found her looking at him. All her attention was for his bruises, with an exaggerated horror straight out of cheap drama. He wondered if in some corner of her mind, she might not be suspecting that there was a hidden camera registering her emotions for the benefit of some enthralled audience. This complex mannerism of hers—this played-at emotion—almost completely concealed her genuine nausea. Certainly, she was unaware of it.

The tape ran out. He stopped turning and pressed the tag end down. He tightened his muscles, testing the set of the tape, preoccupied with his thinking. His eyes continued to focus blindly on the woman, but he had lost himself in what was going on inside his head.

He was thinking that if his conclusions had been correct, then there was no logic governing the universe of Man. When he said "logic" to himself, he meant all that he had ever believed about the eventual triumph of right over wrong; about the eventual reward of proper action and steadfast faith; about the literal existence, somewhere in the operating machinery of the universe, of Justice. A Justice which, if a man only lived so as to deserve it, and contributed his efforts to some equally deserving cause, could not help but give to him and to his cause, all that they well deserved.

He wondered how the intelligent, mature people who had raised him could have permitted him to have taken into his bones the idea that success was a pre-packaged reward, and Justice the cogs and wheels of some metaphysical slot machine which, fed the proper amounts of courage, fidelity and goodness, would in its faithful turn deliver up its prize to a man and his beliefs.

It did not occur to him that the people of a lost cause must necessarily believe in a restoration of past glories if not for themselves, then for their children. He did not stop to think, down in that cellar, that when a political idea finds its military confidence shaken, it turns to a belief in universal moral principles for its hope of deliverance. Individual men may, with insanity or suicide, admit defeat in the only two ways men can remain forever beaten. But causes belong to more than individual men; Man never cries "Enough!"—he waits for the great counterrevolution of tomorrow, which in his heart he sees in wait just under the horizon's rim, as sure as dawn.

Michael Wireman thought it out in detail when he was much older, and needed to, but in that cellar he did not have the time to stop the race of one discovery after another. He felt great changes inside himself, but like a man flung into the midst of a fireworks display, he was so conscious of the ballooning fire and the leaping bursts of sound that he did not stop to think of how the powder had been mixed, or tear himself away from his awe long enough to trace the patient convolutions of the fuse back through the darkness of the years.

All he remembered down in that cellar was his mother, reading stories to him out of the old terrestrial books of fables, and telling him of the good days on Earth.

And this memory irritated him so much to think of again that he scowled like a man in a terrible rage, and shocked Mrs. Lemmon.

"Oh!" she said, "you're not as young as I thought." She was instantly confused, stammering: "That is, I thought you were just a *boy* . . ."

This nonplussed him. Like most people, he had

a mental image of himself that bore only casual relation to his actual physical proportions, but which had a great deal to do with his estimate of himself as a personality. He had a fixed trait, for example, of remembering all faces as if he had been looking up at them. This had no relation to the fact that he was taller than four-fifths of the people he came in contact with. Similarly, his picture of his own face was a caricature; the large, round ears and the sharp jaw dominated it out of all true proportion, leaving only a doughey impression of nose, eyes and mouth to fill out the necessary but characterless remainder. If he had not been marked by those two striking features, as a matter of fact, he would probably long ago have attempted an eccentric moustache, a habitual pipe, a characteristic hair comb, or some other such identifying tag—not as an easy trademark for others, but as a recognition signal to himself.

To be told by this woman—Mrs. Lemmon?—

"I beg your pardon. What *is* your name?" he asked.

"Why—why, I'm Mrs. Evelyn Lemmon."

"Thank you." To be told by this woman, Mrs. Lemmon, that she had seen from his ears and chin that he was not the boy she'd thought him, was a shock. Unless there was more to his face than that? There certainly hadn't been, the last time he'd looked.

What had she seen? The only possible thing could have been his exasperated scowl. And was that an expression she would consider not childish? Certainly even the youngest children frowned and became angry. But not in that particular way?

All right, then. That seemed reasonable. Then a man, as distinct from an aging boy, was someone who had realized that for some reason all he was told about the world as a child was a pack of lies. And this particular anger, compounded of indignation and disillusion, tempered by the humbling memory of all the foolish poses based upon those lies—was that what settled into the faces of men and gave them the cast of what was called maturity? Was *that*—that anger, now permanently mortared into every other emotion—the unspoken password between all individuals who had crossed the threshold from the unreal world of children? Bitterness, that must be jealously nurtured for all time thereafter, so that manhood would not evaporate? Or, at best, a surface urbanity? An easy superficial acceptance of things as they were, masking the never quite smoothed-out corrosions through which must burst, at catastrophic intervals, the lurking need for something better than this armistice with innocence?

Mrs. Lemmon had, of course, continued to stand looking at him while he ignored her. She grew even more uncertain, and impatient for something new to happen. "Is—is there anything else you want me to do?"

"What? Oh—not yet, no," he said abstractedly. He had no plan. He was busy.

A different man might have concluded that his business with himself was now finished. He might have felt that if this was the way the world was, then there was nothing for him but to settle down and take from it as much as he could, for certainly no one else would or could devote any time to helping him. Or he might have felt that, if this was the ugly way of the world, then there existed in it some malignant force which had warped it away from its intended pure goodness. He might then have set out to destroy as much of this malignance as he could, or to set up guards against it. Or he might have withdrawn from the world's concerns altogether, as being the arena of superhuman forces which would sweep over him or gather him up in train sooner or later. He might have chosen to enlist himself at once on the side of what he took to be one of these forces, in the hope of preferment over those inducted willy-nilly.

But Michael Wireman could not quite come to any of these conclusions. For any man who had reasoned this far could have seen how shoddy the world must be, so constructed. But only a man like Michael Wireman could not have gone from this directly to the clutched-at and coveted thought that at least, if he had seen this far, then surely he was a little bit better than his fellow men, who clearly would not be the way they were if they could have seen it, too.

Michael Wireman had no reason to believe he could see anything better than his fellow men could. He had a great deal of evidence all to the contrary. If he had seen it, then surely almost everyone else had, too.

He could only conclude that if everyone else had seen that their maturity was founded on such a pitiable base, then the only reason the world was the way it was, was because they had seen it too late. They had trapped themselves in the habits of years—in the self-crippling hurts, in the narrow, fenced-in lives they had made—and there was no escape. There was only hanging-on, the life too much lived to be made over now, the opportunities lost before they were even perceived, the wrong road travelled much too far. Only the rest of life to be spun out, to be made as comfortable as it could be, warped thing that it was—and the only hope the hope that the children could be so imbued with hope, so instilled with high idealisms that no sorrow and no blow of fate could break them down.

Michael Wireman breathed deeply. He had reasoned it out, in his own way, with his own materials. He was a little surprised, and cautiously ready to be pleased, that he had managed to construct this chain of logic. He went over it step by step, just to be sure, but there was no evidence against it in his life, and a great deal for it.

From complexity, he had come through to great simplicity.

Why, he thought, everyone is just like I am!

He smiled warmly at Mrs. Lemmon, extending his hand. "How do you do, Mrs. Lemmon," he said. "I'm very grateful to you. My name is Michael Wireman. It looks as if now we'll have to help each other."

2

"Wireman . . ." she said vaguely. Then the backs of her fingers went to her mouth. "Oh!"

Clearly, she had recognized the name. And in this real adventure she was having, it could not possibly be a coincidence. She had no idea of the relation of this Wireman to the one she had voted for twenty-five years ago, but it would have been an unthinkable breach of the rules of romance for no relation to exist.

Michael Wireman, of course, could not read her mind. But he could see he had been recognized, and he could see her wavering, not knowing what to do. He had to give her something else to think about. The thought occurred to him that he ought to find out what was going on outside in any case. But how to tie Mrs. Lemmon to him, so that she would not run to the Invaders as soon as she was out of his sight?

"Now, would you please go up and make sure there are no traces of my blood leading up to your door," he said firmly. He had no more real moral justification for remaining free than he had before, but if the world was full of people who had done things they regretted and yet continued to live on, then he was not yet ready to give up and, by so doing, imply that he thought he was right and millions of people were wrong. To say that the drive for simple self-preservation was working in him was to ignore the fact that he was intelligent enough to expect it to do so, and to allow for it in his calculations of his own true worth. It was really quite simple—another simple extrapolation from his one central simplicity.

Mrs. Lemmon had flushed guiltily, mortified by her momentary indecision. "Of course," she said with an apologetic glance at his bandages. "I'll be right back." She hurried up the cellar steps.

Michael Wireman watched her go without worrying whether she would return. He knew she would. It was plain to him that he had succeeded in doing exactly what he had wanted to, and though he did not understand exactly why it should have been so easy, he was gratified to find that it was possible. Obviously, he was giving her something she hungered for—filling some essential space in her life. It saddened him to think that any human being should be so dissatisfied with things that even a man in Michael Wireman's situation would do as a promise of something better. But he would have been less than human if he did not at the same time feel pleased.

But, what now? Where was he going, and if he went, what was to become of Mrs. Lemmon?

He got gingerly back into the Invader blouse. He had to think, now—he had to formulate some satisfactory plan that would cover both of them. But what resources did he have?

And where *was* he going? What was left?

He barely raised his head in recognition as Mrs. Lemmon came back.

"It's all right," she said breathlessly. "There wasn't a sign."

"Thank you," he said. "What're the Invaders doing?"

"I couldn't *see* anything," she said. "But I could hear a number of whistles blowing, and men running along the streets. There were a lot of trucks going by with sirens."

He cocked his head a little. "Yes, I can hear those," he said in confirmation, and was surprised to notice that she was instantly chagrined, as if he had reprimanded her for wasting his time with the obvious. It had not, in fact, been that obvious. The sound, down here, was faint enough to evade the attention of an otherwise preoccupied man.

But he could not be forever soothing her over with explanations. There was not that much time to be spared. And, again, she did not seem to be rebellious. She seemed only conscious of her own shortcomings, real and imagined. How much like I am she is! he thought, particularizing now. What had been a theory about the people of the world was turning into an established fact about specific people. He understood Mrs. Lemmon better, now, and it came to him that if he treated her the way he would have treated himself, and expected of her what he would expect of himself, they would probably get along very well.

"I don't know what all those noises mean," she said tentatively.

"They'll be setting up checkpoints, I think," he said, turning the various possibilities over in his mind and consequently speaking in an abstracted tone of voice. "First they have to establish control over movement through the streets. Then, with each block of buildings isolated, they'll be able to search without having to worry about their quarry slipping away behind their backs." It was all theory to him. He could talk about it impersonally. The effect of his attitude—the seemingly relaxed thoughtfulness, the abstract theorizing, the grasp of military principles which were a total mystery to Mrs. Lemmon—was temporarily lost to him. He was doing no more than a thousand of Mrs. Lemmon's heroes had done before him. His air of knowing what he was talking about was no more genuine than that of a professional actor, reading from a script and as ignorant of what a checkpoint really was as Mrs. Lemmon.

But he was real—alive, right here, and Mrs. Lemmon was, *really* was, right here in the thick of it with him.

Michael Wireman looked at her face idly, and saw that she was staring at him large-eyed, so dazzled that by now it hardly mattered what he looked like or what his personal habits might be.

It was one more in a progressive series of revelations to him, and by now he had come to the conclusion that if he stopped to marvel over each of them, he might be at it all day. It was gratifying—

even exhilarating—to be the object of so much esteem. But he had exhausted his capacity to analyze it all in detail. He was tired, hurt, and frightened. In a way, it was an additional fear to be burdened by so much expectation on her part.

The thing to do was to get out of here, before the Invader net closed down impenetrably. And if he was to keep Mrs. Lemmon from any retribution, the only thing to do was to take her with him.

It was, again, perfectly simple, perfectly direct. He had to leave Philadelphia, quickly, and he had to shape his plans to include Mrs. Lemmon. He did not ask her if she was willing to go. The best thing for her was to go—it did not occur to him to consult with her, and there was no time to inquire into why she was the way she was, or why she would willingly abandon her store, her standing in the community—in fact, all the trappings of her established life.

He would have found she was a widow of long standing, living on the meagre combined income from her husband's insurance and the store profits, that she had been too settled in life for classification, and that she had for years been haunted by the dread that she would not die before the inevitable rebuilding of Philadelphia took away both her store and the brownstone house where she had lived for thirty years. Her nightmare was that she would still be here, but nothing would be familiar—that she would naturally try to pursue her set routine, living in some house she would call home but which would have a different shape from what she knew, that with the condemnation money from the store she would naturally try to age in pursuit of the usual septuagenarian recreations

—bingo, shuffleboard, Florida—when what she really wanted was for everything to be as it was. She wanted to start over, back at the beginning, and if not at the beginning, then at *a* beginning—to move, rather than be moved—to do, rather than be done to—within the limits of her capacity.

She said to Michael Wireman, once, later: "It was knowing there really were people like you that made me read all those made-up stories about people like you," but he was not able to sort his way through that shy declaration until long afterward.

Michael Wireman had no time for the false courtesy of listening when he ought to be doing. He could no longer afford the luxury of waiting for other people to bring him either freedom or death, and neither could Mrs. Lemmon afford to have him feel any other way about it.

3

"But how are we going to escape?" Mrs. Lemmon asked tremulously.

"I don't—" He had almost said "I don't know." But that would have shaken her faith in him, and neither of them could afford that.

And is that my only reason? he thought wryly. It's not, by any chance, that I'm vain of my leadership?

Franz Hammil, he thought, shaking his head to himself, you are with me at this hour.

It was something to think about—something to be put aside now, but not to be forgotten—to be thought out, and weighed, and to be made a permanent part of him—the first of what would probably be a great many doubts, against which every spoken word and action would have to be measured for its content of selfishness.

What he said now was "I don't think that will be impossible." But how *was* he going to get them out, and how was he going to formulate a plan without revealing to her that decisions did not snap instantly into his mind as dozens of impersonators had taught her to expect?

He hit on what seemed to him to be a new and original device. "Suppose we examine the situation," he said with kindly pedantry, as if deliberately taking time to instruct her. He was gratified to see her nod raptly.

"Now, first of all, since we can count on the 'Vaders to be thoroughly experienced in this sort of thing, 'Escape' literally means leaving the neighborhood and the city. Now, to do that"— one thing followed another, quite logically and unremarkably "—we need transportation."

"My delivery truck!" Mrs. Lemmon said delightedly. "I have a number of outside customers for my pastries. The boy services the route every morning, and then leaves the truck in front of the store while he has lunch. The truck's there now."

Michael Wireman nodded. "Very good. Now, what stops us from simply going upstairs and driving away? The checkpoints." True enough. "What are the troopers at the checkpoints looking for? A badly injured man, possibly still in a stolen 'Vader uniform." A change of clothes would be no passport, but no change of clothes would be a death warrant. Michael Wireman looked around. What would the teashop be likely to offer in the way of clothing? "Do you have waiters, or waitresses?" he asked.

"There're two girls."

"A busboy then?"

"No."

"Cook?"

"The pastry chef . . ."

"Do you supply his uniforms?"

"Yes."

"I'll need one."

"Oh, but it'll be miles too big for you!"

How could he disguise that? Pinning it would do no good—and, damn it, it would be fresh and unwrinkled, not looking worked-in at all. He could hardly plan on taking the chef into his confidence and asking to use the one he was wearing now. It might be possible, of course—but too many conspirators could make things awkward. Too many cooks spoiled the broth.

But he had to have clothes, and the chef-sized fresh uniform would have to do. How? That might occur to him in time.

"We'll see," he said, implying with his tone that he already knew, but not missing the flicker of doubt on Mrs. Lemmon's face. "Now—the crucial part of the identification will be my physical condition, correct?"

She nodded, while he wondered what to do. He could not cover up his nose, or the rest of his face.

"Well, what *about* my physical condition? What do they know about it? They—" And here, perhaps, was the only leap of intuition in all this train of thought. And not much of a leap was required, at that. "They know my injuries are several hours old. They won't examine fresh accident cases." It all came together now, and Michael Wireman was properly surprised to see how much could be gained by simply stopping to take a situation apart.

"What will happen is this: you, Mrs. Lemmon,

will go running out into the street, shouting for
help. There will have been a certain amount of
noise and smoke in your kitchen, and an oven will
seem to have had a mild explosion. The 'Vaders at
the nearest checkpoint, or, more likely, some mu-
nicipal policeman, will come running. They'll find
me, with most of my chef's uniform burned off,
lying unconscious in the kitchen. They won't find
the chef—he'll be down here, with a gag in his
mouth if necessary. And they won't find a fire or
serious damage; there'll be no excuse for them to
empty the place or search it for additional hazards.
But I'll have gotten the oven door right in my face
and chest, and they'll have to take me to a hospital.

"Now—" It had been going quite well, up to
now. Abruptly he had to stop and get more
information:

"Do the 'Vaders issue identification cards to the
general population or just to their civilian employees? Something with a physical description, a pho-
tograph, fingerprints, and an official seal?"

"They—they used to, but it's been years since
the last general issue. Lots of people have lost
theirs by now. They're not replacing them or issu-
ing new ones."

"Just letting it taper off, eh? Good. Then I'll be
carrying the chef's wallet in my pocket, with no
identification in it beyond a social security card or
whatever other useable papers he has.

"They'll send for an ambulance. You'll follow
along behind it, to arrange for my care and sign
the compensation forms. Make sure you do all the
talking to everybody official who comes with the
ambulance, make sure none of your help gets a
good look at who the ambulance crew carries out
of the kitchen. On your way to the hospital, stop

off and buy me some civilian clothes; put them in an overnight bag, and have them sent up to my room. Arrange for me to have a private room." He smiled suddenly, conscious that he was overpowering her with his rapidfire directions. "Do you think you can do all that? Good!

"Now. As soon as they're through setting my bones and sewing me up, I'm going to ask to go home. I want a formal discharge from the hospital. They might grow suspicious if I slip out. I don't see why they'd want to give me a general anesthetic, so I ought to be mobile quite shortly. If I do have to stay there overnight, that'll complicate matters—but not if your real chef doesn't get out. Do you think you can keep him locked up down here. Any means will do, as long as it works without fail."

"Yes—I—of course. I'm sure I can."

"Good. Now—wait outside the hospital for a half hour after they tell you I'm out of the operating room or wherever it is they set broken noses. Wait around to the left side of the building—park in the first block on the first street to the left of the building—and then, if you don't see me, come back here, make sure the chef's still immobilized, and then go back to the hospital in the morning. Don't try to call me by telephone—switchboard girls have only one thing to do for entertainment on duty. Just wait for me, and don't worry. I'll be out." No need to make an alternative plan for himself if something went wrong at the hospital. "If I'm not out by nine-thirty or so, take the truck and drive—" Where? "To the mountains. You won't like the dissidents much, but there'll be some other people down there in a week or two. You'll find they're pretty civilized."

The C.S.O. liasion with Hammil. Michael Wireman's mouth crooked wryly. What kind of a world would Hammil make of Earth?

There'd be a few desultory battles. Newsted and Ladislas might prod Hammil into action, but they could not make more of him than there was. The Invaders knew what to expect. One or two engagements and Hammil would be through, the dissidents scattered once more. The C.S.O. would pull out in disgust.

What kind of a world would Hammil make of Earth? A solidified Invader one, with permanent large garrisons and a constant program of precautionary checks on population loyalty. And what would become of Mrs. Lemmon?

"But—but where are we going if everything does work out all right?" Mrs. Lemmon asked.

"Where?" Well, yes—where, and to do what? "Well," he said with a sigh, "I don't suppose there's really anyplace but the mountains, is there?"

He looked away from Mrs. Lemmon for a moment, his thoughts turned inward once again. He remembered raving to Hobart this morning about how easy it would be to take over from Hammil. Was it really that easy? The whole world? Make a plan, stand at the right place at the right time, make the right move, and everything falls into place? Then what was all the agony about?

4

He came out of the hospital in the morning carrying the empty overnight bag, dressed in the poorly-fitting civilian work clothes Mrs. Lemmon had brought, and swung down the street until he came to the truck. She was sitting in it, biting her lips nervously, her eyes sleepless. He smiled at her from behind his mask of neat, professionally done dressings. "Well, here we go, Aunt Evelyn," he said cheerfully, "off to visit my Cousin Francis in Stroudsburg and let me recuperate from my accident."

It was a beautiful morning. The sunshine and his evidently good spirits would do their work on her soon enough. She had obviously been under an enormous strain, and needed every bit of help he could give her. "Would you like me to drive? This thing doesn't have power steering, does it?"

He took her place behind the wheel and studied the instruments carefully before starting.

"The pastry chef is going to wait down in the cellar until noon," she said in a strained but proud voice. "Then he's going to work loose from his ropes—I weakened the knots for him—and turn me in as a traitor. He asked me to have you remember him when you come back to Philadelphia."

"You've done very well," he said gratefully. He was surprised and pleased to have her work things out so neatly, in spite of the fact that she had allowed less time than he liked for getting clear of Invader radio patrols. He'd been troubled by the thought of having to leave the chef bound and gagged, to be discovered God knew when.

It was his first experience with subordinate amplification of an executive plan he had outlined, and it was a great relief to have encountered it.

"But what did you tell him, for Heaven's sake, to make him cooperate like that? After all, I came up behind him and knocked him on the head, he woke up tied in a bundle down in that—in the—cellar. . . ."

"I told him about you," Mrs. Lemmon said simply. "About how you were going to go up in the mountains and get things organized, and how you were going to come back and throw out the Invaders. That is what you're going to do, isn't it? Don't they deserve it, after what they did to you?"

Michael Wireman blinked. It did not occur to him that, for Mrs. Lemmon, plot threads ran very simply from A to B, and injustice was always punished. And, assuming he did what he now saw he must, could she ever be proven wrong? Hadn't her training as an adventure romance devotee already proved worthwhile?

"Something like that," he said, pointing the truck down the broad street which would eventually turn into the highway that wound up into the mountains. It was amazing how much she had constructed out of nothing more than encountering him and listening to him say a few words. And how close her construction came to the truth—close enough to be mistaken for it, he imagined.

"I knew it!" Mrs. Lemmon said, as proud of herself as she was of him, but conscious that her pride in herself stemmed directly from his impetus. "I could tell the moment I saw you. I said to myself: 'That's a strong man. He knows what he's doing.'"

This was so patently ridiculous that Michael Wireman writhed with embarrassment for her. He tried to think of some way to disabuse her of her illusions, but at first he saw no choice between deliberately failing, in order to open her eyes, or giving her a long and boring lecture on his life as he saw it. Perhaps he could evolve some simple mechanism —some phrase, or gesture, that would shut this kind of thing off before it was well started. He wouldn't have to explain it—he would only have to use it, and have it marked down as some kind of forgiveable personal quirk.

But he had not evolved it yet, and so he merely sat glowering, annoyed at her for not being able to see through him, when he himself could see through himself so clearly.

And it was really all so very simple, he thought. They were all in this world, they were all conscious that it was the sort of world that had to be comprised with if it was to be lived in at all, and, under their compromises, they didn't like it. And if one of them happened to be in the right place at the right time to change the world, to give them all something better—not something perfect, necessarily, but something better—then it was up to that one of them to do it.

It was all as simple as that. One thing led directly to the next.

Michael Wireman drove on. He could not be corrupted, because the world had nothing to offer him but its own extinction.

He could not be dissuaded, because he would know, afterwards, that he had traded the world's opportunity for a mess of glittering words, and the thought of going to his deathbed with that for a memory was enough to make him listen to no one but himself.

He could not be frightened, because nothing less than death could change him now. He had gotten down to what he really was, and seen it; he had gotten down to what the world was like, and understood it; he could always find himself and the world again. And even death could only put an end to him—it could not swerve him.

When he was somewhat older, and many other

things as well were different for him, he asked himself whether he had really understood himself and the world, or whether he had only convinced himself he had. But by then his way of looking at things could be proven to have been successful. So he concluded with a wry smile and a shrug that, whichever the truth was, it was too late for him to change now.

SEVEN

1

The two-lane asphalt county highway wound and dipped in response to terrain features a more important road would have graded away. The sun was in the west; its light flashed on and off the windshield as the bakery truck followed the road, and made confusing patterns in the scuffs left over the years by the wiper blades. Although the highway was climbing through forested slopes, the trees had been cut back and the shoulders were flanked by scrub bushes and weeds, so there was no shade. It was hot in the truck; neither window would wind all the way down.

They had been traveling all afternoon. Michael Wireman had to keep his torso rigidly twisted into the one relatively bearable position, and squint past the sweat and pain in his eyes. Mrs. Lemmon sat beside him with her hands in her lap, smelling more and more perceptibly of ladylike talcums and sachets. Perhaps, he thought, the swelling in his nose was lessening. Perhaps not.

185

He glanced at her from time to time, marveling at the invarying somnolent cast of her expression, wondering if perhaps she were simply between episodes of their drama. When he looked at her, and found her utterly unchanged each time except for the growing perspiration patches on her dress, his mouth was apt to draw into a fond smile briefly.

They came to a T-shaped intersection and turned left, past the State Police station and its parked gun-carrier. The flag hung unstirring at the top of the pole. There was fresh gravel covering the patch where the police car had burned. There were no troop trucks. Two Invader soldiers in caps were filling the gun-carrier's fuel tank from jerricans. Mrs. Lemmon's hands pressed down on her thighs.

"Look toward them, Mrs. Lemmon," Michael Wireman said gently. "You would be expected to glance at people doing something purposeful."

"Oh, yes," she agreed quickly, and turned her face with a fair approximation of naturalness, though her feet remained pressed rigidly against the floorboards. Michael Wireman turned his face too, enough to register normal innocent reaction, not enough, behind Mrs. Lemmon, to show the ravaged detail of his stitched and mottled features. He reached his left hand down and touched a fingertip to the pistol lying under his thigh.

The soldiers looked over casually, their eyes mere glints in the shadows under their cap bills, and resumed their work. Then the truck was past them, and Mrs. Lemmon sighed. In a few hundred yards, the road curved—fourth-class, now, narrower and lumpy—and the command post vanished from the rearview mirror. The trees closed in. The truck was suddenly deep in woods, a ditch and upslope to the right, a ditch and then downslope to the left, with only an occasional reflector post and no guard-rails.

"We'll go on for a while, but we'll soon be walking," Michael Wireman said. He had no idea of where Hammil might be now, but he thought he could find the camp up the mountain. Even if Hammil had shifted his force out of it in anticipation of an Invader area-search, someone would have been posted to watch it, and would report them. Hammil would have them gathered in. That would do. Michael Wireman began to survey the sides of the road up ahead, looking for a place where the truck might be abandoned in some degree of concealment.

He saw a rust-eaten mailbox on a leaning iron pole, and then a dirt ramp leading up into a rain-ravaged gravel track the width of a car, disappearing at an angle up the slope with no sign of its destination. Slowing, he studied it for recent use, and there were tire-tracks, but only those of a civilian car. With a nod for Mrs. Lemmon, he turned the truck up the track which, he could then see, led up to a switchback that continued the climb up the face of the mountain. He eased the truck onward, stones and twigs rattling in its fender-wells, branches squealing along the sheet-metal of its sides, the engine beginning to labor on the relatively mild upgrade, and twisted the wheel over to make the switchback. A spasm ran through the muscles over his ribs, but was over soon enough.

As they made the turn, with only a narrow view of the mailbox below them, the gun-carrier drummed past it on the road, hurrying from the direction of the command post. If anyone in it saw wheelmarks superimposed on old ones, the vehicle did not slow or stop but continued on its unknown errand.

Mrs. Lemmon bit her lip. Michael Wireman moderately increased the pressure of his foot on the accelerator, and soon there was nothing but thick growth to either side of them and, farther up, perhaps the beginning of the next switchback. He was mildly surprised Mrs. Lemmon hadn't asked if he knew what was ahead, but he was beginning to accept that she would not ask such things of him.

He calculated when the roof of the truck might begin to show above the line of the next switchback, and stopped. Easing open his door against the roadside bushes, he slid through the narrow gap and crawled up the steep slope beside him, worming through the bushes, pushing with the sides of his boots, and pulling on firmly-rooted growth one-handed, holding the pistol. He brought his eyes up behind a screen of vegetation. There was nothing to see, at first, but the up-angling continuation of the roadway and the slope of the next elevation, but then he saw an open and unweathered carton that had held a clip of small-arms ammunition, lying beside a fresh tire track together with a chewing-gum wrapper.

He looked back down over his shoulder. Mrs. Lemmon had slipped over on the seat and was looking up at him, her expression waiting for news and instructions. He braced himself so as not to fall while holding his weapon away from the soil, put his fingertip across his lips, and then motioned from side to side, palm down, so that she repeated the hushing signal to him, nodded to show understanding, and sat back to wait.

He climbed the next elevation, and saw a State Police car parked hull-down exactly as he'd left the truck. He watched it, and all around it, until he was sure it was unmanned, crossed the road quickly, and climbed the last slope. Raising his head, he saw two men in police uniforms. One was an Invader and one was shortish, stocky, and blond. They were in a fringe of trees and scrub vegetation at the upslope side of the track, separated from each other by about fifty feet, and were crouched down behind cover. Their faces were turned toward a badly deteriorated clapboard farmhouse set back among abandoned vegetable gardens and a front lawn gone to hay.

The slope in the immediate vicinity of the house was shallower. Whoever had built here had originally cleared about five acres of forest and gotten plowable ground out of it, but almost all of it had been given back to second growth at some time before the rest was abandoned. Beyond the original clearing, the mountain steepened again, tall old pines rising out of head-high deciduous growth, full of shadows, with the sun beyond the mountaintop and sinking. At about this time of day, Michael Wireman saw, anyone looking out the west windows of the house would be staring into the high contrast between the dazzling sky and the dark vegetation.

But he was facing toward the east windows. From time to time the two policemen glanced at their watches, and over at each other. A loudhailer lay on the ground beside the squatting Invader, and the Earthman had a satchel that looked as if it might contain grenades. Each of the policemen had an automatic rifle ready in addition to his holstered sidearm. The Invader had binoculars, and was systematically scanning the windows of the house with his head inside a bush to shade the lenses.

Michael Wireman studied the house. There were

no signs of life. But there was a suspicious opacity about the broken and dirty windows on both storeys. It seemed unlikely that an abandoned house would have been left with all shades down, or, if it had, that all of them would still be rigidly fastened, unflapped and untorn by winds over the years, undamaged by whatever stones or other vicissitudes of time had breached most of their glass. Nor would it be likely that ordinary house-shades would produce the particular impression of featureless darkness you would get if you used military blankets to black out a house so you could function in it overnight.

Michael Wireman shifted his main attention to the two policemen again. They were looking at their watches a little more frequently now, and the Earthman was tensing and untensing his thighs so that he bounced a little. He was a bad soldier. But, then, he was more of a policeman.

There were only normal forest sounds, and the usual forest heat where the sun could penetrate. Michael Wireman became conscious of the various pains in his body, but he could also see that this static situation would not continue much longer and, indeed, with last satisfied references to the time, the Invader looked sharply to a specific quadrant up the mountainside and beyond the farm-house, while the Earthman reached into his satchel and began jiggling a gas grenade in his palm while working his jaw furiously.

A flare winked into green light above the trees where the Invader had been looking and he instantly shouted "Come out with your hands up!" through the hailer while shattering the remains of the upstairs windows with a quick flirt and stutter of his automatic weapon. Simultaneously, and with a showy deftness, his partner overhanded three grenades one after the other in a row that burst and laid a screen of boiling yellow thick vapor across the front of the house to the level of the second storey. Then he picked up his quick-firer and shot into the smoke. Meanwhile, the Invader was shooting one-handed, shouting unintelligibly into the loud-hailer at high volume, and holding it so the firing of his gun was picked up by the microphone and amplified, until the face of the house echoed with tumult.

Michael Wireman pushed with his feet, hitched his elbows up over the lip of the slope, braced his forearms, and shot both policemen in the back, aiming between the shoulder blades and a little below. The Earthman simply pitched abruptly to his side. The Invader said "Aww!" within range of the loud-hailer, and then died. Michael Wireman's elbows burned where recoil had scraped them against the ground.

He was up over the edge and darting immediately to the satchel and the discarded weapons; he had them and had crossed the lawn and flung himself against the north base of the house before the gas cleared enough for him to be seen. He had held his breath; even so, his eyes and nose were full of it. But something much like that had been done to them before, in training, except that the Centaurian sergeant had grinned and struck him in the stomach to make sure he got heavy exposure. "You will live, likely," the man had said, and indeed Michael Wireman was alive now, belly-crawling rapidly along the crumbling brickwork foundation toward the far corner of the house, his ribs aching, his eyes streaming but staying open enough to watch for what the diversion had been intended to cover. He pulled the half-empty satchel up next to his side and cradled the Earthman's weapon in his arms. He felt the indicator with his thumb and learned the clip was nearly expended, but he was not relying on direct firepower.

He heard a scuffling sound at an upstairs window, and then a thud and a grunt around the corner of the house. Looking quickly, he saw that Newsted had jumped down on the side away from the policemen and was holding up his arms to take the weight of a man wrapped in bandages with old blood on them, who was being lowered down knotted in a rope of blankets. Other men were at the windows, and as soon as Newsted had laid the first man semiconscious on the ground, another was thrust out and received. The operation was proceeding with swift concentration, while other men fired sporadically from the upper front windows into the trees where the police had been.

The gun-carrier burst from the forest upslope, crashing through a screen of brush, an Invader squad strapped upright in the jouncing afterbody and firing toward the house. Michael Wireman jumped up, kept his body behind the angle of the house, and flung grenades into them until the carrier swerved out of control and stalled, and the men in the upstairs windows shot the squad and the choking driver to pieces.

Michael Wireman shook his head. He sighed, softly.

Newsted looked at him. Michael Wireman raised his rifle. Newsted shook his head and grinned wolfishly; he lowered his own gun. "So *you're* the hero," he said, indicating the fallen Invaders.

Michael Wireman looked at the gun-carrier, canted over at an angle, its deck surmounted by the detritus of dead Invaders; at the bundles on the ground at the base of the farmhouse, who were Earthmen too stricken to walk; he felt his own body, which could barely stand, and whose face hurt almost unbearably. "Oh, yeah, I'm the hero," he said.

2

While they loaded the wounded into the weapons carrier, he went down and got Mrs. Lemmon. He drove the bakery truck as far as the stopped State Police car, and then without comment he ushered her out of the truck and climbed straight across to the waiting troops, so she wouldn't see the bodies of the two men in State Police uniforms. Perhaps she wondered about the car and what it was doing there, and where the policemen had gone, and perhaps she didn't—it was hard to say, since she didn't comment.

But short of making the police car disappear, or short of showing her the bodies and explaining he personally had shot them, in the back, and why, he was doing the best he could. He let it go at that, and she for her part didn't seem to wonder. She simply stopped, with an "Oh!" when they got to the gun-carrier now full of wounded Earthmen.

In fact, looking at the unspeaking men draped as best they could over the afterbody of the car, and the dead Invaders lying heaped to one side, and the blood all over everything, and Newsted and the others standing next to the gun-carrier, staring at Mrs. Lemmon as surely as she was staring at them, Michael Wireman did not explain that the men were the non-walking wounded from the assault on the police station, or how it was that she was with him, or anything else. It was too complicated. "Let's go," he said, and they went, he and Mrs. Lemmon and the rest, the gun-carrier lurching over the ground, with Newsted walking ahead to guide the vehicle through the trees, and Michael Wireman and Mrs. Lemmon and the rest of the party, who could walk, walking, and it occurred to Michael Wireman that many supposedly complicated situations could be resolved by simply saying "Let's go."

A woodpecker went *rat-a-tat-tat* among the trees, somewhere. No one noticed.

3

They came, at last, to Hammil's camp, well up the slope, hidden from the air by trees. It was more populous than the camp Michael Wireman remembered from a few days ago, but, then, Hammil had started to attract men from independent bands already. At first they were met by troopers, but soon enough Hammil himself appeared, booted and crewcut, wearing a uniform top. He stared incredulously at Michael Wireman. "Well! Our wandering boy has returned!"

Looking at him, Michael Wireman thought of the test, and it occurred to him that he and Hammil had something in common. He was not at all sure that it made any difference. "Yes," he said.

"Well, what do you want?" Hammil said.

"I think we'd better talk."

Ladislas Danko had come up to join Newsted. He stood watching Michael Wireman carefully, next to Newsted.

Hammil said: "There's nothing to talk about. If you want to be a trooper in my army, I might think about that. Anything else is out of the question."

Michael Wireman looked around him. Mrs. Lemmon was off with the camp women, making whatever she could of that. He was still wary of showing her a rough side. Satisfied, he turned and shot Hammil through the head. The man dropped cleanly dead.

He did not explain. He simply watched Newsted and Danko. For a moment, Newsted's rifle had twitched up. But it had sunk back down. Danko had not even done that much. Which was just as well, because Michael Wireman had planned to let them kill him if that was the way of it; he couldn't hope to get out of the camp alive if Newsted or Danko objected.

"Jesus Christ!" Newsted was saying.

Professor Danko looked down at Hammil lying huddled on the ground. He looked back at Michael Wireman. "Now what?" he said. Beyond them, men were starting to react, but when they saw Newsted and Danko continuing to converse with Hammil's killer, they didn't know what to do, and so did nothing.

"Well, now we begin," Michael Wireman said, and, slowly, Newsted and Danko nodded.

EIGHT

1

Ralph Wireman came carefully down the gangway from the C.S.O. transport's grounded hull. One of his nearly translucent hands slipped grudgingly down the rail. His feet shuffled forward, testing the way.

He could feel Thomas Harmon steadying him with one hand on his elbow. Perhaps because he was lately very much conscious of his physical helplessness, he resented Harmon's tactful help. Harmon, after all, was not so young himself. He ought not to be so unfeeling as to give help—particularly, effective help—when none had been asked for.

And yet what was it but kindness and consideration? What was it, really, but Tom saying wordlessly, "I know how it feels to be you." And wasn't that the greatest gift one person could give another?

He had to stop—to change the subject of his thoughts. Emotion came too easily to him, in these

latter years. Everything he experienced became
poignant to him, as if with the approaching end of
physical experiences the emotional perceptions
sharpened to a nearly unbearable degree. Is that
why, he wondered, the old are so outwardly
stolid—so chary of more than a bleak smile, or a
strangled laugh—because if they permitted themselves to express the storm of their feelings, they
would shake their frail bodies apart? Only careful
little outward smiles, and, inside, laughter, laughter
—a world of joy; if we could hear each other's
thoughts, would all the world be wreathed in clouds
of tumbling joy?—would the world sing with our
delight at each small thing in it? But we cannot
hear each other's thoughts, so perhaps it's only I
who have this unheralded discovery to explore?

He resisted the pressure of Harmon's arm, and
Harmon stopped with him, halfway down the
gangplank.

Laughter, Wireman thought—no guffaws, no bel-
lows of risibility, no sneaking titterings, but the
happiness of children discovering the world. And
will I now discover the world anew? Sitting quietly, so as not to break the web of it, showing
none of what I feel as I send my mind out, out into
the past and see it through my newly sharpened
inner senses? A new horizon? A new adventure,
playing out its wonder in my thoughts, while on
the outside there is nothing but a furrowed smile
to show? A smile, or tears, perhaps. Tears are
easier than laughter. Tears need no gust of breath,
as laughter must though breath is short—tears do
not crack the muscles of the back or make the jaws
ache when the jaws are sore-gummed from the
artificial teeth—yes, old men's or old women's
gentle tears; these, too, are safe; not grown men's

sobs, but children's tears; not children's tantrum-cries but children's tears upon that moment when they learn that, in all justice, children, too, can fairly die—those are the tears that we regain when we are very old.

I must look closely at whatever old men I may meet, Ralph Wireman thought. It may be that in the end we cross the borderline of human flesh's ability to contain emotion; that for all our care, the moment comes when control is lost. That may be death. And that may be our afterlife; each of us going down into that private world—laughter for those who have a memory of joy, sorrow for those who have a memory of grief; our pasts, our lives, reduced to one great quintessential pang, and then, as our sense of clocks and days is left behind, there's our Eternity. . . .

"Earth," Ralph Wireman said, looking at the pines. "Earth, Tom."

"There's Michael," Thomas Harmon said.

Ralph Wireman looked, narrowing his eyes and pushing his head forward on its neck to lessen the distance between himself and the vague vertical brush-stroke of dull green confronting a sharper, broader white blur that were all he could make out across the landing area.

"He's talking to Captain Lemby."

"I see him," Ralph Wireman said irritably.

With a clack of boot heels and a rattle of arms, an honor guard assembled at the gangplank. "We're being waited for, Ralph," Harmon nudged him.

"All right. I'm as familiar with protocol as you." Too late, Ralph Wireman remembered that he had learned to see Thomas Harmon in a new light. He glanced guiltily over his shoulder, but his old friend's face was not hurt—only impatient.

I must—I must not let people see me falter, Ralph Wireman forced the thought. I must not take up too much time between one move and the next, I must not speak sharply, I must not introduce an element of strain . . . I must be someone to be reckoned with, for a little while longer, rather than someone to be accounted for.

But it was becoming increasingly hard for him to so much as hold that thought. To obey it required fantastic effort, and it was all too clear to him at his age that any effort could reckon its worth in inverse ratio to its expense. Strange, he thought, remembering how easy it had been for him to spin out his soliloquy on Age, that my mind should be so lucid at constructing metaphysical neverlands, and so clouded at dealing with the world that is.

He shook his head querulously. He had been shuffling down the gangplank all this time, and now there was the boy, standing in front of him. Lemby, the Plenipotentiary assigned to negotiate with Earth for the C.S.O., was hanging back, and the honor guard—an ill-assorted group of native Earthmen in C.S.O. fatigue uniforms with home-made insignia sewn over the C.S.O. markings—was keeping its eyes front. Because all these people were here, but not participating, and only the boy was speaking to him, and because only at this short range were his eyes of any use as resolving instruments, it was to Ralph Wireman as though all time and space had suspended their forward progress. He and the boy stood in a moment without time, and consequently all time—all their past, all their lives together—were of a piece, with no part pushed aside by some more recent part, but all towering like a monolith, so that what he and the boy were, at this moment, were something infinitely greater than the one day, one hour, one moment cross-section of an individual gripped by life, which men in ordinary parlance call a man.

"Michael," Ralph Wireman said.

"How are you, Father?" Michael answered.

"I'm—well. Your mother—" He gestured vaguely backward. "She's resting from the trip." He gestured again. "You remember Thomas Harmon?"

"Very well. How are you, Mr. Harmon?"

"Fine, Michael. I'm glad to see—"

Yes, Ralph Wireman thought, letting his ears shut momentarily, Thomas Harmon was impressed with Michael and what Michael had done. He had spoken about it a great deal, aboard the ship on their trip from Cheiron, where they had first been put in custody in an uncomfortable hotel and then, inexplicably, their status changed because of something Michael had done here, offered luxury transportation to Earth.

But Ralph Wireman was not impressed with what Michael had done. Anyone could get what he wanted, if he negotiated from a position of strength. To get more, one had only to grow stronger, until the point was reached where even whims were automatically translated into ironclad demands by those conditioned to the feel of that strength. Thomas Harmon knew that as well as anyone. But he did not really believe it was an inflexible law of the human universe. He found it impossible to believe that it could work for Michael Wireman as well as any other man. He had given the boy his opportunity, because his reason told him so, but he was astonished by success because his emotions had not concurred in the decision.

And by that margin of unbelief in your own

intelligence, Ralph Wireman thought, you're not
as fit to lead men as I am, Tom. But it hardly
matters anymore—a few more weeks, or months,
and there'll be an end to it. We'll negotiate some
sort of demarcation line between our sphere of
interest and the C.S.O.'s, and then there'll be an
election, and it'll be all over for us. Then we'll sit
in the sun, and make our ways toward Eternity,
and you'll go to what your life has made for you,
and I will go to mine, where we shall never meet
each other except in dreams of our own making.

It was what Michael had become that impressed
Ralph Wireman, because he knew that anyone
could not become anything he wanted, but only
what was in him, and he had never thought that
Michael had it in him to be his own kind of man.
On Cheiron there had been no sign that Michael
had the great thing a leader had to have—self-
confidence; the knowledge that men were not one-
tenth as wise or sure as they pretended to be—not
one-twentieth as purposeful in their own minds as
they seemed to be; that they knew they needed
direction, and automatically followed those who
chose to lead the way; and that with any reasonable amount of common sense and education, any
man of reasonable intelligence could lead them
toward something at least as good as what they
had—certainly better than what they would have
if they were left to shift for themselves. So long as
that man took care to establish a guiding philoso-
phy from which he did not deviate, he would have
no difficulty. There was the rub—how many men
were born into each generation with the will to
conceive a direction and follow it all their lives?
Such a man, of such a rare type, must necessarily
know his stature above other men. And all his life,

he had to keep a careful balance between this vital self-awareness of his unique gift, and an overweening, fatal sense of godlike predestination. On one side of the balance lay benevolence. On the other, tyranny. Just that, to explain the riddle of the great men of human history, and nothing more, Ralph Wireman knew.

But to think that Michael—his Michael—had come to it!

"How did it happen, boy?" he asked, breaking in on whatever it was someone else was saying to Michael. "Where did you learn?"

Now that he was within Ralph Wireman's range of vision, Michael could be examined and judged in one experienced glance.

He had not hardened much, Ralph Wireman saw. It seemed that he was simply not going to become the lean, quick man his father had been. All he had done, really, was alter the way he set his feet on the ground. But to accommodate his new, sure stance, every muscle in his body had had to tense or relax into a new relation with his bones, and this had a subtle effect on his outward appearance. A man's features are defined by the way light strikes the hollows and prominences of his face; so, too, with the rest of his body. The boy's head was carried differently on his neck from the way Ralph Wireman remembered it; the light struck his eyes and nose at a slightly changed angle, and the resulting new light-and-shadow pattern gave him a new visage.

"It didn't seem that I had any choice, Father," Michael answered him, and though it thrilled Ralph Wireman to see the way his son had understood him, and replied, when the others about them were mystified, still it was a strange answer, and

Ralph Wireman wondered if they had really understood each other.

He worried about it as he and Harmon were introduced to other members of Michael's group, because he did not have to devote his interest to learning anything about them. They were all of them part of a classic pattern—the useful members of the overthrown predecessor's entourage, or else new men promoted from the ranks, to fill the classic functions of interim government: men without polish or practice, who did important work well not because they trained for it but because their entire natures were so concentrated as to make that particular work psychically important to them. Monomaniacs, a more stable regime would have called them, and removed them for their mania and all the other faults no polished officialdom could tolerate.

It was a pattern as old as history: this Newsted, the arm of law and discipline, the extension of one facet of Michael's necessity as an irregular leader; this Hobbs, this Morganson, this Lopert, this Ladislas—the stolid, mature balance weight against the young commander's impetuosity. . . .

"Ladislas Danko!" Ralph Wireman gaped.

"Old friend," Professor Danko rumbled, gently clasping his shoulder.

"I was never your friend!" Wireman shrilled, twitching his shoulder away.

"I had thought, perhaps—" Danko shrugged and turned away uncomfortably. It came to Ralph Wireman that his old opponent had been appalled to see him so old, and had tried, in his best way, to declare the old arguments at an end. And now he was embarrassed by Wireman's rudeness.

Well, let him be, Ralph Wireman thought. It

was too bad that men could not all have control over each human intercourse, but the fact was that in any act between people one had to gain control over the others, or no one's purpose would be served. Danko had, for all his kindness, been trying to force their relationship into a path of his choosing. It was necessary for Wireman to have declared that he would not follow it.

"Father," Michael Wireman asked softly, "have you helped Earth by playing that sort of game with Professor Danko?"

"Helped Earth? Of course I—" He checked himself sharply. That was not the point at all. The point was, who was the leader here? Once that was established—once each of them had made his attempt at directing things among them, thus clearly establishing relative ascendencies, then the government of Earth could proceed unhampered by further jockeying.

Or had all that been done already?

"Michael—have you seized the Presidency from me? You haven't left a place for me, is that right?"

Michael said, "It's hard to tell, Father."

Ladislas Danko began: "The legal position is extremely unclear. There is first of all the question of whether the C.S.O. treaty with Hammil had any status under International Law—that is, whether any part of it had any actual effect in conferring the leadership of Earth on Hammil. Again, disregarding the treaty, there is the question of whether Hammil acquired status independently of it, under the view that his actions constituted a *coup de main* against the Free Terrestrial Government in Exile, assuming the coup to have some *de jure* standing. Accepting for the sake of argument, that Hammil was titular head Terrestrial government, then there is the question of whether Michael received that title as his legitimate heir following a trial by arms in which he killed the late General, or whether he was restoring order on Earth in the name of the Government in Exile—that is, upholding your authority—or usurping it for himself, or merely carrying out a counter-revolution basing its claims to sovereignty on *force majeure*. Furthermore. . . ."

But Ralph Wireman was not listening. Nor was he, he found, overtaken by shock or disappointment. He had known all along, of course, that his position was as fragile as paper, and that inevitably it would drift away in the first clean wind to sweep across the face of Earth. But to have it be Michael —to have it be someone he did not understand, whose motives he could not reckon, whose guiding precepts he had ever examined—not to know, in short, where his authority had been passed on—left him confused and unsure of himself.

I used to know what I was doing, he thought. I used to plan things and accomplish them, most of the time. Don't I remember something—years ago—aboard the ship—about *not* wanting to go on with it? But every man has his bleak times. He loses faith in his plans. But only for a little while. He goes on. Who's to say why I changed my mind?

Did I change my mind? If I can't remember, did it happen, or do I just think it did? Who's to say I used to know what I was doing? Who's to say things were the way I thought they were? The only thing I have to guide me is my memory. Is my memory perfect—or does it only seem that way to me? Has my mind rewritten the past, so that all the jagged facts are mossed over and made to look greener, more pleasant than they really were?

Oh, Lord! Ralph Wireman thought, I am the prisoner of my brain, and my brain is human— only human, trying to make things pleasant, trying to make it possible for me to live with myself, trying to arrange things so that my last thought will be joy instead of sorrow—Oh, how important that's become to me! If I had only known when I was younger! It's too late, now—too much of the past is behind me. How can I, now, change it? Or have I changed it—have I, indeed, slurred over truth, so that the timeless mindworld into which I go will be a false, a hollow thing in which I will not rest?

"Mr. Wireman," Captain Lemby said to Michael, not to Ralph, "we have to settle things. These fleet units can't be spared forever. The Invaders have been pushed off balance, but we have to establish a cordon quickly now, all along this volume of space, to fend them off while the main body hits them from the other flank."

Michael looked patiently at Lemby. "I'm sure that's true, Captain," he said. "But while you're thinking in terms of hundreds of light-years of distance, and fleets of battleships, you must remember that it was my father who made it possible for you to clear this sector. He's just learned that his job is done. A man doesn't like to carry that sort of burden for years and then, when he lays it down, have no one give him time to draw a breath. Your fleets will keep—let's walk quietly over toward my tent, and by then, I'm sure, we'll be ready to return to politics."

The boy laid his hand gently on Ralph Wireman's arm and said, "Let's walk together."

                        *   *   *

They sat around the long trestle table in Michael Wireman's tent, and Ralph Wireman watched drowsily, seeing his boy deal with the C.S.O.

"See here," Lemby said, irritated and uncomfortable. "We agreed to certain things—the blockade, the supplies, the transportation for the members of the old Government in Exile, the recognition of your status. Now, you've got to give us something back. Trading concessions, reparations payments—*something*, for Heaven's sake!"

"Well, yes," Michael Wireman said. "We're grateful for your help. But without us, you wouldn't be winning your war with the Invaders."

"*Our* war? It's your war, too!"

"Then, we're allies. Do you consider it honorable to try to gain an economic foothold on our territory, in return for your having done what is only expected of friends and allies? You pointed out, Captain—it's your war, too. You'll get a great deal of benefit out of it. As much as anyone ever gets from a war."

"Wireman, you'll get a great deal of benefit if we open our blockade and let the Invaders sweep through here again! You'll wish you had us back."

"You can't do that, Captain," Wireman said, shaking his head slowly. "What did you tell your people, back home, when you began this war? That you were in economic conflict with a rival power—or that you were coming to the rescue of oppressed Earth? I know your government, Captain. It's a good government, but it thinks that the ordinary people must be given some noble excuse to cover the harsh realities of life. Your government thinks the common people don't know what life is. No, Captain—you can't let the Invaders re-take us, because your people would rise in indignation and throw your officeholders out."

Lemby hunched over the table, his shoulders ridged with muscle, and raised one hand to point. "Mr. Wireman—"

"I'm sorry, Captain. I wish for your sake that your government hadn't chosen a career officer for a political errand. I think they chose you because they expected this would happen, once they found out Hammil had been displaced. Now they'll be able to take their spite out on you by breaking you of your rank. They'll probably offer you your choice of disgrace or a suicidal command on the battlefront. I know which you'll choose."

Lemby stood up quietly. "You call your shots well, Mr. Wireman. Earth is fortunate in you."

Michael Wireman looked up. "I intend to do my best."

2

Ralph Wireman stood beside the boy, and looked down from the mountaintop. He could not yet grasp this new thing in Michael. He could not understand.

"I learn a little every day, Father," Michael said, standing wearily. "A little more about how I have to act, and what has to be done. It's all mechanical. Anyone could learn it."

"That's not true," Ralph Wireman said quickly.

"It's true. I'm sorry, Father, but what you think of as a very difficult business to learn is nothing more than what every baby has to learn the first time it encounters another baby. It has to decide what is rightfully its own, and what belongs to this other individual, and how to come to an agreement on that point. Being a baby, it first tries to take everything for itself, as does its opponent, and then by fighting and crying and by tearing some things to bits, the lines are painfully drawn. Then, when the baby is grown, it remembers the injustices it committed, or tolerated on itself—the meannesses, the deceits, the wasteful combats. It suddenly realizes that it made mistakes, and committed treacheries, and it must then somehow live with the memory of its own imperfections. But it must live. So it goes on, and in trying to account for the past, it warps the present, so that, when it is older, it sees that error breeds error—shame begets shame, and treachery is as much a part of the human soul as faith. And then it must learn to live with that, and that's all. A man cannot lead himself. He can only do what he can for others, because he can see them as they are, instead of what they must think to themselves they are, and so we help each other."

Ralph Wireman took the boy's arm. "You believe that? You're talking to me, now, Michael. I've known great men. I was a great man myself. A great man knows he's great. He can't function without that knowledge. If a man is a leader, somehow, but doesn't know he's better than the rest, he has no justification for the things he does—the arbitrary decisions he must make. It's impossible for a man to be like that!"

"I'm sorry, Father," Michael Wireman said. He turned around gently, so that his father could follow, and they began walking back toward the tent where Michael Wireman's mother was resting, waiting for the helicopter that would take them all to the city, where they could begin the business of living as a family for the little time that was left in Ralph Wireman's generation.

THE END